The Windmill Café

Autumn Leaves

Poppy Blake is an avid scribbler of contemporary romance and romcoms. When not writing she loves indulging in the odd cocktail or two – accompanied by a tower of cupcakes. The Windmill Café series follows the life and loves of Rosie and Matt in the glorious countryside of Norfolk. Why not pop in for a visit?

🐦 @poppyblakebooks
📘 www.facebook.com/poppy.blake.395

Also in this series

The
Windmill

Autumn Leaves
Café

Poppy Blake

A division of HarperCollins*Publishers*
www.harpercollins.co.uk

Harper*Impulse* an imprint of
HarperCollins*Publishers*
The News Building
1 London Bridge Street
London SE1 9GF

www.harpercollins.co.uk

This paperback edition 2018

First published in Great Britain in ebook format by
HarperCollins*Publishers* 2018

A catalogue record for this book
is available from the British Library

ISBN: 978-0-00-832437-7

This novel is entirely a work of fiction.
The names, characters and incidents portrayed in it are
the work of the author's imagination. Any resemblance to
actual persons, living or dead, events or localities is
entirely coincidental.

Set in Birka by Palimpsest Book Production Limited,
Falkirk, Stirlingshire

Printed and bound in Great Britain by
CPI (UK) Ltd, Croydon CR0 4YY

To Mum and Dad; I know you would be so proud to see my name on the cover of a novel

Chapter 1

Rosie surveyed the Windmill Café whilst she waited for her chocolate and pecan brownies to bake. Even without the burble of her customers' cheerful chatter, the room still resonated with warmth, comfort and contentment. However, Rosie felt far from contented and comfortable because she knew she needed to broach the thorny subject of that night's approaching escapades with Mia before she exploded from an overdose of anxiety.

'So, what do you think of the blackberry and apple roulades?'

'I think they're amazing! They're definitely going on the menu for the Autumn Leaves Hallowe'en party on Saturday,' declared Mia, cramming a third mini Swiss roll into her mouth and rolling her eyes in confectionery ecstasy before crumbling into a fit of giggles.

'And the pumpkin and treacle tartlets? Do they make it onto your list?'

'Absolutely, and the apricot and cranberry brownies, and the gingerbread with lemon icing, and the red velvet cupcakes with the raspberry coulis that looks just like blood! You know,

I really wish you'd reconsider my *fabulous* idea to hide eyeball gobstoppers inside the Boston Scream pie.'

'Health and safety, Mia. Don't you think we've had enough contact with the food inspectors to last us a lifetime? Okay, so that just leaves us with the punch to finalize.'

Rosie leaned over the huge copper jam pan she had been adding spices to all day. She inhaled a deep breath, savouring the heady fragrance of warm red wine, cinnamon sticks and cloves that sent her taste buds tingling. She gave the dark crimson liquor a stir before sampling it, gasping as the alcohol hit the back of her throat. Maybe if she downed a couple of glasses of the lethal brew she would find the courage to confess her swirling trepidation to Mia.

'Well, if it tastes as good as it smells, we're onto a winner,' said Mia. 'And we're definitely having the hot chocolate with marshmallow ghosts and the green slime smoothies for the kids. I take it, then, that you've also vetoed my idea to float plastic spiders in the pomegranate cocktails?'

'Yes! Of course I have!'

Rosie rolled her eyes in mock chastisement, but after what had happened at their Summer Breeze party in August, she was even more nervous than usual about hosting this celebration of all things scary – she didn't think she could cope with a second drama. It hadn't been her fault that one of their guests had been poisoned, but she'd still insisted on triple-testing every recipe for their Autumn Leaves party before it was granted a place on the menu, stipulating that only the most delicious, mouth-watering creations would be allowed to feature.

The celebration was also billed as a farewell bash for Mia, her friend and fellow baking fanatic, before she embarked on her foray into the field of outdoor sports. She was going to train as a zip wire instructor at the outward-bound centre, Ultimate Adventures, over the winter season when the café was only open at the weekends. Rosie knew she would miss Mia's daily dose of chirpy banter, but she consoled herself with the fact that Mia was following one of her dreams. And anyway, they would still be able to meet up in the local pub, the Drunken Duck, whenever they wanted to partake in that trio of female solace; cocktails, cake and gossip.

She slid the last batch of cupcakes onto a wire rack to cool and plunged the baking sheet into a sink of hot soapy water, relishing the loud sizzle. She scrubbed the tray clean, dried it, and returned it to its allocated place in the drawer below the oven, before reaching for the antibacterial spray to wipe down the marble countertops one last time.

Rosie saw Mia smirk and shake her head in exasperation but choose to say nothing, and her heart ballooned with gratitude. Her friend understood the reasons behind her constant battle with the cleanliness demons, and the way she was unable to relax until every surface of her beloved café was spotless and sparkled under the overhead lights. She returned the spray to her box of deodorizing goodies, shoved her copper curls behind her ears where they burgeoned like inflated candy floss, and untied her apron strings, watching in amusement as Mia did the same.

'I'm loving the autumnal theme you've got going on today, Mia! Black cats and witches' hats are a perfect choice for our

Hallowe'en bake-a-thon,' she said, referring to her friend's very loud apron.

'And what did you think of the pumpkin one I wore yesterday?'

Rosie thought back to the previous day when she had struggled to keep a straight face as Mia – Queen of Quirky Culinary Attire – had produced an apron bedecked with pairs of pumpkins divided by what looked like courgettes, giving the unsuspecting onlooker pause for thought. She had politely declined Mia's offer to make one for her so they could present a united front, insisting she preferred to stick with the Windmill Café's signature aprons made from plain peppermint-coloured linen and embroidered with a very tasteful white windmill.

As Rosie performed her final check of the electric plugs and switches, the pirouette of unease that had curled through her veins all day tightened and she knew she couldn't ignore her mounting apprehension any longer. She needed to just come straight out and say what was on her mind.

'Do you think there is any way *at all* we can get out of going wild camping tonight? I've still got a long list of things to organize for the Autumn Leaves party, not to mention having to be around in case the remaining guests in the lodges and the shepherd's hut need me for anything.'

Mia grinned, a glint of mischief appearing in her dark mahogany eyes.

'You'll need to come up with a much better excuse than that, Rosie! Matt and Freddie have been looking forward to this expedition for weeks. Anyway, how can you possibly consider giving up the chance to spend a night under the stars with Norfolk's very own version of Bear Grylls? It's the perfect opportunity for you to cement your relationship.'

'Mia, I keep telling you, Matt and I are just friends!'

'Friends who worked together to save the Windmill Café from certain disaster. If you and Matt hadn't turned supersleuth and uncovered who was responsible for poisoning Suki, then we wouldn't even be having this conversation. Did Matt complain when he came to our aid in our time of need?'

'No, of course he didn't, but...'

'So, now we're repaying the favour. Matt needs us to go with him and Freddie to balance out the numbers. Only four of our lodge guests have signed up for the *Wild Camping and Medieval Myths* expedition; that's all three of the guys, and Brad's girlfriend Emma is coming too. Without us tagging along, it would mean Emma would be the only woman, so this way it's a good mix with Matt and Freddie as our extremely hunky guides. Perfect!'

Mia removed her apron, shoved it into her handbag and slotted her arms into her white denim jacket which she had hand-embroidered with a garland of custard-yellow buttercups. More hippie than yuppie, Mia had definitely been born in the wrong era, with her love of all things flower-power, from the daisies in her hair to her gem-encrusted sandshoes.

Rosie adored her best friend and partner in culinary creation. She was well aware that the only reason she had been able to progress from forlorn florist to contented café manager was down to the eternally optimistic support of Mia Williams. It had been weeks since she had tortured herself with the memory of discovering her ex-boyfriend Harry rolling around amongst the chrysanthemums in their little flower shop in Pimlico with one of their bride-to-be clients. Her new home in the white-washed windmill with the peppermint green sails had turned out to be the perfect place to put her life back on track. She had moved on.

In fact – and she didn't intend to admit this to Mia any time soon – she had even started to toy with the possibility of dating again. Just because she'd had her fingers burnt once didn't mean she should avoid every encounter with a cosy log-burning fire for the rest of her life, did it?

However, there was still one thing she needed to work on and that was her attachment to her good old friend and enemy – bleach. No matter how hard she tried to contain her ever-present urge to clean, she just couldn't relax until she was satisfied that not a single germ lingered anywhere in the café waiting for its chance to pounce on the gullible. She suspected that her obsession with hygiene required the attention that only a professional therapist could provide – especially after the heightened anxieties her recent brush with a potential food-poisoning scare had caused.

'Right. I'll let you go upstairs and get packed and I'll see you over at Ultimate Adventures at seven o'clock. I know I don't have to say this to you, Rosie, but I will anyway. Don't be late! It's a good hour and a half hike to where Matt and Freddie want us to set up camp for the night. And don't forget to bring a torch ... and maybe a few of those brownies too! Bye-ee.'

Rosie waved Mia off in her cute little cream Fiat 500 then

locked the Windmill Café's French doors behind her. Mia was right. They did have to return the favour for the kindness and support – not to mention the Poirot-esque tenacity – with which Matt had helped her hunt down the person responsible for the poisoning scandal that had almost brought her idyllic Norfolk countryside sojourn to an end. If she had lost her job at the café, then she would also have lost her home.

So, it was thanks to Matt Wilson, the handsome and intrepid owner of Ultimate Adventures, that she was still in Willerby, baking scones, roulades and tartlets for the hungry hordes who were about to attend the inaugural Autumn Leaves party on Saturday night.

Rosie made her way up the spiral staircase that led to her studio flat above the Windmill Café. She had only made a lacklustre start on packing for her night under the stars. More like night*mare* under the stars, she thought as she groaned out loud. How on earth had she got herself into this? She really wasn't an outdoorsy kind of a girl, the sort who relished the chance to commune with nature. She was more Countess of Cupcakes than Connoisseur of Camping.

Oh well, all she had to do was tip her hesitation over the parapet and launch herself into the unknown – again!

Chapter 2

Rosie parked her car alongside Mia's Fiat in the gravel car park next to Ultimate Adventures' reception lodge. Set against a dense arboreal backdrop, and sporting a wide sun-bleached veranda, the outward-bound centre's office looked more like a wooden ship floating on an emerald ocean. It had taken Matt months to persuade her to participate in one of the various activities on offer there and finally, in order to avoid the very scary looking zip wire ride, she had succumbed to his powers of persuasion and joined him on a field archery shoot, which she had to admit she'd enjoyed. However, she had no doubts whatsoever that the same thing could not be said for the treat he had in store for them that evening.

Twilight was tickling the canopy of trees overhead and the woodland had taken on an eerie feel that sent goose bumps scooting across her forearms. She grabbed her borrowed rucksack from the boot of her car and made her way towards the group of people gathered underneath a pool of amber light next to the store room waiting for instructions.

'Hey, Rosie, great to see you!' exclaimed Freddie, stepping

forward to greet her with a fist bump before seeking out Matt and handing over a crisp ten-pound note.

Rosie rolled her eyes, but was gratified that the gesture at least meant Matt had retained his faith in her. She had no intention of letting him in on the details of her earlier conversation with Mia, or the fact that she was only there because Graham, the Windmill Café's owner, had asked Matt to arrange the personalized expedition for the guests currently staying in the luxury lodges on the site next to the café as part of a themed week of activities.

Four members of the group, two men, Rick and Phil, and a couple, Brad and Emma, were self-confessed obsessives when it came to local legends and folklore; they were members of a club back in Manchester called the Myth Seekers Society, dedicated to the pursuit of all things mysterious and spooky. The mere mention of ghost-spotting was another one of the reasons Rosie had baulked at joining them. No wonder only one of the women in the party had decided to accompany them on their trek, and judging by the way Emma was hanging onto Brad's every word, that was probably because she couldn't bear to be apart from him for even one night.

Rosie envied Helen and Steph, their remaining lodge guests, whom she suspected would at that very moment be wallowing in their heated outdoor spas with a glass of something fizzy. In fact, she had seen the glee on Helen's immaculately made-up face as she waved off her husband, Rick, and his friends, before rushing over to Steph's lodge for a session with the local beautician who had just arrived with her case full of treasures. Oh, how she wished she was with them. She couldn't remember the last time she'd had a manicure.

'Ready for one of the most exhilarating nights of your life?' asked Matt, his familiar mischievous grin going some way to improve her flagging spirits.

Dressed in his Ultimate Adventures uniform of black jeans and bicep-hugging black T-shirt with purple logo, he looked every inch the ruggedly handsome Action Man. His dark blond hair had been teased into surfer-dude tufts, and his determined jawline sported an attractive smattering of stubble. Maybe a night in the great outdoors chasing mythological creatures wasn't going to be such a terrible experience after all, thought Rosie, as a ripple of attraction sped through her veins.

'Absolutely!'

'Now why don't I believe you?' Matt laughed. 'We're lucky – it's forecast to be a mild night with no rain expected, but the three most important rules of any wild camping expedition are preparation, preparation, preparation. So, here, put this on, it'll keep the chill off.'

'Thanks, Matt.'

Rosie accepted the black waterproof jacket, emblazoned with the Ultimate Adventures logo and lined with a thick purple fleece, and she instantly felt protected from whatever the meteorological gods might decide to throw at her.

'Hi, Rosie. I have to confess, I wasn't sure whether you'd turn up!' giggled Mia as she huddled deeper into her Siberian goose down jacket and pulled a thick Inca-inspired woolly hat over her ears.

Rosie mock-glared at her friend who had been so keen on joining one of Matt's expeditions. Why, oh why had she listened to Mia and agreed to hunker down for a night under the stars in a bivouac in the East Anglian wilderness?

She thought of all the things she could be doing at that very moment, like delving into the any of her numerous glossy cookery books, reading about each recipe's origins, its ingredients and its method of preparation. In troubled times, these tomes of culinary marvel had been her best friends and she'd often wondered why someone hadn't thought of bottling the inky smell of freshly printed cookery books and offered it for sale to all fanatical bookaholics.

Alternatively, she could be soaking in a hot bath filled with the luxury bubbles her sister Georgina had given her for her birthday, anticipating the delicious delights she and Mia were planning for the Autumn Leaves party on Saturday night, only six days away.

But no, here she was, freezing her butt off on the edge of a pine-fragranced forest, preparing for a night under canvas – all for the dubious pleasure of watching dawn break over the horizon through an ancient stone archway at the centre of a crumbling old priory! So what if the medieval building was supposed to possess certain healing qualities? She didn't have rheumatism or rickets! And was she really expected to believe that if a chunk of the stone was ground up and heated in milk it would cure a migraine in an instant? How did that golden nugget marry with the equally extolled myth that 'disaster shall strike any man who removes a stone from its resting place'?

Was she crazy? Had she completely lost control of her senses?

Rosie glanced round at her fellow extreme campers – eight of them all together – in various stages of excitement for what lay ahead. Unlike her and Mia, every one of them had opted in advance for the full 'Bear Grylls' experience and would have no canvas screen between them and the great beyond. Obviously, Matt and Freddie were veterans of wild camping, having led several expeditions for Ultimate Adventures, but even they hadn't enjoyed the experience with a side-order of mythical exploits.

'Hey, Rosie! Hey, Mia!' Emma smiled as she came over to join them, her jade-green eyes bright with anticipation for the approaching adventure. 'I'm so glad you decided to swell the numbers in the girls' team! Which part are you looking forward to the most? The hike to where we're camping tonight, or the actual sleeping under the stars part? Or, could it be the bit where we get to experience the mystical aura of the medieval stones?'

'None of the above,' muttered Rosie, wondering if Emma was winding her up.

It was all well and good for her to wax lyrical about the approaching experience – she was the only one who got to snuggle up in the muscular arms of her hunky boyfriend so, in Rosie's book, that didn't count as enduring physical hardship. Emma had already declared that the gruelling three-mile trek across the countryside, through woodland and brook, field and beck, was going to be one of her and Brad's most romantic experiences. In fact, now that Rosie was able to scrutinize the couple's attire more closely, the love birds even *looked* like they were about to embark on a marathon, dressed from top to toe in matching figure-hugging Lycra and hi-tech breathable Gore-Tex.

'What could be more exhilarating than curling up with another human being, sharing bodily warmth, with nothing between you and the stars?' asked Brad, hitching his rucksack further up his broad, muscular shoulders so he could snake his arm around his girlfriend and drop a kiss on the top of her elfin-style haircut. At six foot three, he towered above everyone, but he wore his impressive bulk lightly. 'Maybe you should try it sometime, Rosie? Matt's just told me that you and Mia have decided to sleep in a tent. You don't know what you're missing. Emma and I have camped in the open air all over Europe. Oh, and remember that night we spent on a rooftop in Marrakesh, babe?'

'That was amazing! The best night ever! The stars were so bright it felt like you could actually reach out and touch them. Just perfect! You've *got* to go to Morocco, Rosie.'

'At least it's warm there,' she mumbled before she could stop herself.

Rosie pulled the hood of her jacket tightener round her chin and resisted the urge to rub her palms together and stamp her feet for fear of looking like a petulant toddler being forced to partake in a dreaded activity. This trek was the reason the guests were staying at the Windmill Café lodges and Graham would be expecting her to promote the experience so she plastered a smile on her face.

'Tell Rosie and Mia about our trip to Athens in May, Brad,'

said Phil, stepping into their conversation, his ever-present Pentax bouncing against his multi-pocketed camouflage jacket in his enthusiasm to enthral the group with the details. A first glance, Rosie thought he carried a few extra pounds, but on closer inspection she realized that every pocket had been stuffed with a myriad of orienteering and camera parapher-nalia. She managed to quash a smile as Phil continued. 'You'd love the Acropolis, Mia. It's got this unique mystical power I've never felt anywhere else. I'm hoping to go back there with Steph so I can show her what I mean.'

'I think Steph might have other destinations on her list before Athens,' laughed Rick, the chairman of the Myth Seekers Society and the person who had organized the trip to Norfolk. 'Especially if you're going to drone on and on at her like you did with us about the type of scaffolding the ancient Greeks are supposed to have invented. Oh, and you might like to avoid all topics relating to the Greek waste management system, the poor air quality in Greece's largest city, and where to buy the cheapest film for your camera, if you don't want Steph to slit her wrists from boredom.'

Rosie stared at Rick, taken aback by his rudeness and the jeering tone he had used to speak to one of his friends and fellow enthusiasts. What shocked her the most, however, was that no one challenged his boorish behaviour.

Nevertheless, when she chanced a quick glance from beneath her eyelashes at Phil, she could see his cheeks had reddened and his shoulders drooped a few inches. He detached himself from the group, lined up a few photographs, and then took out his notebook to record some notes with the stub of a pencil he kept behind his ear. Rosie's heart gave a nip of sympathy and she resolved to have a chat with Phil about his hobbies and, if she got the chance, to ask him about Rick's offensive attitude.

'Right, is everyone ready for an Ultimate Adventure?' asked Matt, coming to stand in front of the assembled crowd like Bear Grylls' younger brother with a beaming Freddie as his right-hand man.

'Yes,' chorused the group, minus one voice – Rosie's.

'Let's go, then!' declared Matt before leading the way along a well-trodden footpath through the woodland that encircled the outward-bound centre.

Rosie took up the rear, just behind a chattering Mia and Freddie, with the enthusiasts up front with Matt so they could get the most from his running commentary on the variety of flora and fauna that could be found in the local area.

Once she got into her stride, Rosie realized she was actually quite enjoying herself. She had never even considered taking a walk through the trees at night – for obvious reasons – and this was one way of being able to do that safely. And October was a good month to experience everything that the Willerby countryside had to offer because all around her the autumnal woodland architecture excelled itself. Ancient oaks stood tall next to sturdy sycamores dressed in leaves of russet brown, burnt orange and dark gold. Vibrant red berries dangled from the branches of the rowan trees like fairy lights and tiny toadstools poked their heads through the carpet of mulch adding their pretty faces to the visual medley.

When the group eventually left the woodland behind them

and started their hike across the fields to where they would be camping that night, Rosie sighed with pleasure. The vista laid out before them, bathed in the silvery light of the moon, was enough to impress even the most jaded of sceptics. She had to accept that, once again, Matt had been right about challenging herself to try new things. She experienced a sudden surge of energy and picked up her walking speed to a trot to join him at the head of the group.

Maybe this wild camping expedition was going to be fun after all, she thought. Until she stubbed the toe of her unfamiliar hiking boot on a large stone protruding from the path and was catapulted to the ground with a loud *umph*.

Chapter 3

'Enjoying yourself?' asked Matt, a cheeky glint of amusement dancing in his bright blue eyes as he stuck out his hand to help her back up.

'I was.'

Rosie grimaced as she tried to untangle a sprig of dried-out grass from her bushy hair – glamorous, it wasn't! Now that they were out in the open, the calm night air of the forest had morphed into an insistent breeze sending a helix of leaves and twigs into their path. Her fall had knocked the stuffing out of her and sent her spirits southwards; her shoulders ached where the straps of her rucksack dug into her skin, her nose and eyes watered from the constant slap of cold air, and there was a blister forming on her big toe – and they still had another mile to go until they reached the clearing where they would set up camp for the night.

She met Matt's eyes, recognizing the gleam of an outdoors fanatic. Clearly, he was in his element, enjoying whatever nature decided to throw at him, the more challenging the better. If she could have turned around and trudged back to the cosy warmth of the Ultimate Adventures office she would

19

have done so without any hesitation. The only thing stopping her was the fact that everyone else in the party was having the time of their lives, not to mention the enthusiastic chatter about what kind of ghosts they were likely to come across before they arrived at their destination, Garside Priory, the most haunted place of all.

'What in God's name possessed me to listen to you and Freddie and agree to this torture?' Rosie rolled her eyes and tried to laugh, but her voice sounded more like a hysterical hyena.

'What's the matter with you? It's character-building!'

'That's complete marketing drivel spouted by masochistic morons from the comfort of their air-conditioned desks. It's soul-destroying, that's what it is! How can spending the night in a cold, damp, miserable environment with a bunch of outward-bound fanatics and dedicated ghost hunters possibly change my personality for the better? Now, on the other hand, if we had found ourselves lounging in a Jacuzzi, sipping iced cocktails and listening to the faint drift of jazz music then I could see how *that* might persuade me to build better relationships with my fellow sufferers.'

'They're a strange bunch, aren't they?' said Matt, lowering his voice as he fell into stride next to Rosie to allow Freddie and Mia to take the lead.

'I'm so glad you said that. Did you hear the way Rick spoke to Phil earlier?'

'Seems like our chairman of the Myth Seekers Society has let some of the power go to his head. Before you arrived, he had a real go at Brad and Emma for not studying, and committing to memory, the detailed file of notes he'd prepared for everyone on the local folklore of Norfolk, and more specifically, the many myths surrounding Garside Priory. In fact, he was so annoyed at them he even threatened to introduce an exam before allowing members to put their names down for future Myth Seekers trips. Brad apologized, but I thought Emma was going to launch an attack for his jugular. He's not an easy man to like, I have to say.'

'I agree. Would you believe he asked me what the annual turnover was of the café? When I told him that Graham was the owner, not me, he accused me of lacking ambition, saying I should make it my business to know everything about the organization I work for, no matter how small and "insignificant". It was the first time I've seen Mia lost for words and she's avoided him ever since for fear of being unable to resist the urge to spike his coffee with a generous dose of rat poison.'

'What's his wife like?'

'Oh, Helen's lovely! She visibly cringed when Rick was interrogating me about the café's finances and five-year plan. You should have seen the relief on her face when she waved everyone off tonight. If you ask me, I think she was really looking forward to some alone time. Rick doesn't speak to her in that arrogant tone he reserves for everyone else, but he does tend to talk over the top of her, mainly to contradict what she has to say. It's embarrassing, but I guess she's just become used to it.'

'And Phil's wife?'

'Steph. I like her, she's like a mother hen protecting her mate. She's the only one I've seen challenge Rick when his comments become overtly obnoxious. In fact, she took him to task only this morning when he called Phil a wimp for wearing thermals and telling him that real men brace the elements! I thought they were going to come to blows! I'm not sure why Phil is so often in the firing line because he seems like a decent guy, if a little obsessed with his camera. I swear he sleeps with that thing around his neck!'

'Rick wants to be careful,' joked Matt as he helped Rosie over a style into a field filled with golden corn swaying languidly in the breeze. 'Hasn't he ever heard the story about the worm who turned? Or, perhaps in his case, the worm's wife! All this boorish behaviour might one day come back to bite him. I'm glad at least someone is prepared to stand up to him.'

'Helen and Rick don't have children, but Steph and Phil have three, ranging from five to eleven, so she seems to treat Rick like a naughty schoolboy, or more precisely, the playground bully. Sadly, the bully is not yet ready to learn about the consequences of his taunting. Steph was telling me earlier that she intended to make the most of the trip down here because it was the first time she and Phil had been away without the children. She and Helen have got an evening of prosecco and pampering planned,' she added wistfully.

Matt laughed. 'Okay, Little Miss Intrepid, I'm pleased to announce that your torment is almost over. Look, there's our campsite for the night! Come on, last one there makes the coffee!'

Rosie shook her head and took off in Matt's wake towards a clearing at the edge of the woodland they had been hiking around. Of course, she was no match for Matt, and by the time she arrived her heart hammered its objection to the sudden exertion and her breath came out in ragged spurts. Maybe if she survived the night out in the cold she should really think about joining a gym.

'Okay, this is the best area for the sleeping bags, and over here is where we'll build a fire,' said Freddie, unpacking the essential items for a night under the stars from his rucksack.

'Brad, Emma, would you like to collect the water for our coffee from the stream at the other side of those sycamore trees? Rick, Phil, can you scavenge for some firewood? Rosie, Mia are you okay to erect the tent?'

A tickle of guilt meandered into Rosie's chest, but was swiftly eradicated when she thought of the alternative. The one concession Matt had agreed to was that she and Mia, and Emma if she changed her mind about sleeping outdoors when she knew what it entailed, would be afforded the privilege of sharing the only tent for the night. At least it would provide them with shelter from the unpredictable weather that could descend on the Norfolk countryside without warning.

Feeling like she was the star turn in a comedy sketch, Rosie spent a humiliating thirty minutes helping Mia to put the tent up and by the time they had finished – to a smattering of applause from a smirking Matt and Freddie – she wished she'd opted for the open-air version! With her cheeks burning, she scanned the darkening horizon for any sign of Brad and Emma making their way back with the water so they could prepare their evening's rations and a welcome tin mug of freeze-dried coffee. It wouldn't be the Jamaican coffee they served at the Windmill Café, but she had to thank God for small mercies!

As Rosie took a seat next to Mia in front of the fire that Freddie had coaxed from a few twigs without any difficulty, waiting in thirsty anticipation for the scorch of hot coffee to course through her veins, she allowed her thoughts to twist over the last two months. After the poisoning incident had been cleared up, the café had gone from strength to strength and Graham had reduced his references to the unfortunate matter from daily to weekly. October was the end of the tourist season, so the opening times had been reduced to take into account the decrease in custom.

Mia was excited about her new position as trainee zip wire instructor. It meant she could stay at home and still work on her popular travel blog which was increasing its traffic every week. After her gap year, Mia had returned home with a bucket list of dreams she wanted to fulfil and was working her way through them at a rate of knots – baking maestro, zip wire expert, travel writer, camping aficionado, loyal friend. Rosie would miss her cheerful presence at the café, not to mention the daily dose of laughter and the strong bond of friendship they had formed. She knew she had Mia to thank for introducing her to Matt and Freddie and bestowing her with a second chance at happiness after the debacle with Harry.

But, as she smiled a 'welcome back' to Brad and Emma who were giggling at some private joke, she wondered if she was being premature in her assessment of her new-found contentment. There was now, she was sure, a higher-than-average risk that the new Windmill Café manager – herself, Rosie Catherine Barnes – was about to die of hypothermia, or be mauled by the spirits protecting the Garside Priory, or be eaten for breakfast by a shaggy dog called Black Shuck.

'Coffee?'

'Thanks, Emma,' said Rosie, accepting the metal mug of hot coffee. She took a tentative sip, allowing the warmth to seep into her veins, watching the tendrils of steam wind skywards in a languid spiral against the ink-black sky.

'Anyone want to try one of the Windmill Café's signature apple and caramel muffins?' asked Mia, producing a large Tupperware box from her rucksack.

The group devoured every morsel as though they'd been hiking through the fields and woodlands for days on end instead of for just over an hour and a half. Abiding by the rules of wild camping, Mia collected the paper cases and stored them back in her rucksack to dispose of later.

'Hey, Phil, are you going to put your pinny on and do the washing up?' called Rick, a smirk playing around the corners of his lips as Rosie cleared away the mugs. 'I have to say, I'm surprised you didn't elect to stay with the ladies back at the lodges. Weren't they planning to whip up a few chocolate cupcakes before adjourning to the hot tub for a sweet sherry and an early night between the soft cotton sheets. Tell me, do you prefer cotton or silk?'

'Rick, give it a rest, will you?' said Brad, unable to meet their designated leader's eyes but compelled to intervene after seeing the mortification on Phil's puce-infused face.

Rosie saw a flash of mischief float across Rick's expression as he slotted his legs into his sleeping bag and smiled at Phil who visibly shrank from the laser beam of malice concentrated in his direction. Phil's shoulders were hunched into his khaki jacket and his fingers fiddled nervously with the strap of his camera which he hadn't removed since they'd left Ultimate Adventures. He reminded Rosie of a shy meerkat – one who preferred not to poke his head too far above the parapet before returning to his hiding place out of the spotlight. With his straggly beard, his thinning hair and his pale beady eyes, his pasty appearance spoke to the excessive amount of time he spent in front of a computer screen practising his photographic hobby.

'Hey, why don't you read one of your bedtime stories for us, Phil? Lull us all to sleep with an onslaught of ennui? You really should think about pursuing a new ambition. How long have you been writing that new book of yours now? You do know that no one's going to publish it, don't you? I started to read your last one a few months ago and Helen said I was asleep within five minutes – comatose more like.'

Matt cleared his throat before interrupting the one-way conversation. 'Okay, everyone, if we want to be up before dawn for the trek to the Garside Priory, we need to bed down and get some rest.'

He took some time to scrutinize the area where they had made camp, making sure every utensil they had used was wrapped up and stored securely in his rucksack, then he checked to ensure everyone else had followed his example.

'Nothing is to be left behind. This is private land and the landowner has only granted us permission to camp here on

26

the strict proviso that we take everything away with us and camp as unobtrusively as possible.'

Rick stretched out in his sleeping bag, his fingers laced behind his head.

'I've been wanting to see the Garside Priory for years. I must admit, there's something very mystical about being able to watch the sunrise through the eastern arch. Maybe we'll all be endowed with special, magical powers. What do you think, Brad?'

'Wouldn't say no to a few magical powers,' sniggered Brad, snuggling against Emma's spine to share her bodily warmth as the temperature began to drop steeply.

'What's so intriguing about a crumbled old ruin?' asked Rosie. 'I'm not sure I can be bothered to hike over the fields just to watch dawn break through a stone archway. I might just stay here and wait for you to return.'

'Well, I'm definitely going,' laughed Mia. 'I love all this folklore stuff.'

'Sorry, Rosie, I'm afraid that's not an option. We have to stick together, mainly for safety reasons, and I had to promise Giles, the landowner, that none of us would go off-piste and explore on our own.' Matt cast a suspicious glance in Rick's direction as he wriggled into his sleeping bag. 'It was one of his stipulations before granting his consent for us to camp here. The hike will only take about twenty minutes, maybe thirty, depending on the weather in the morning.'

'You don't want to miss it, Rosie!' interjected Phil, dragging out a guidebook from one of the many zipper pockets in his canvas jacket. 'To watch a new day break over the horizon through a medieval church arch is a spiritual experience you'll never forget.'

'Oh no, here we go. A recital of the various myths surrounding the priory according to our resident humdrum author, Philip G. Brown,' groaned Rick, rolling his eyes theatrically.

'I was just going to...'

'What myths?' asked Mia, sitting up a little straighter, her kohl-ringed eyes swinging between Phil and Rick.

'One of the most fascinating aspects of Garside Priory, in my view, is the reference to the possibility that there's a concealed stone circle in its grounds, hewn from local material and buried over the centuries,' enthused Phil, flicking through the pages of his guidebook until he reached the photograph he wanted to show to Mia.

'And why do you think it's there?' asked Rosie, still unconvinced that the possible presence of a circle of stones was worth getting up before dawn for.

'Well...'

'It's only a theory,' interrupted Rick, who, despite his eagerness to prevent a lengthy academic lecture from Phil, was quite happy to give one of his own. 'If there *was* one there, it could have been a religious or ceremonial meeting place, an astronomical observatory, or maybe a pagan ritual site. But, Mia, the legend you *do* need to be aware of is this – there's a possibility that the priory was built from stones that are cursed.'

'Cursed?' whispered Mia, her eyes widening as she twisted a lock of her dark glossy hair around her index finger, the silver from her numerous rings glinting in the moonlight.

Rosie saw that despite his earlier criticism of Phil, Rick was clearly enjoying himself in the role of raconteur and was accustomed to holding the floor.

'One legend recounts that disaster shall strike if any person removes even a chipping from one of the stones.' Rick flashed a stern warning glare around the gathering. 'And one of my favourite stories is that anyone who falls asleep inside the priory walls "will die a heinous death or go mad or become a poet" – let's face it, none of us want to morph into Phil, do we?'

A smatter of giggling erupted from the direction of Emma and Brad.

'What time do we have to be up in the morning for the final push, Matt?' asked Phil, when his facial colouring had returned to its usual pale and wan. 'We can't risk being late.'

'We'll need to leave here at about six o'clock. It's an easy thirty-minute hike which should get us there in good time for sunrise. I've set my alarm so no one needs to worry. Get some sleep and I'll wake you with a brew,' said Matt, Norfolk's answer to Action Man himself.

Chapter 4

'What time is it?' croaked Rosie as she peeled back her eyelids and realized the dawn chorus was already well into its second verse. She rubbed her eyes and, despite her head feeling like a bulbous watermelon, she marvelled at the fact that she had slept at all.

'Mmm?' groaned Mia, rolling over to face Rosie, her hair more bird's nest than Sunday best. 'God, my head aches. I feel like I spent last night indulging in a boatload of the Windmill Café's autumn punch!'

Rosie groped for her watch, shaking her head to clear the lingering fuzziness, and her stomach gave an unexpected lurch. 'Hey! It's seven o'clock! Mia, we've missed the trek to the priory. They've left us behind!'

'What? No way!' cried Mia.

Rosie crawled out of her sleeping bag, grateful that she'd chosen to sleep fully clothed. She unzipped the flap of their tent, irritation at being ditched gnawing at her gut. She had no doubt whose idea it would have been to leave the two silly girls behind. As she peered out, Mia joined her, resting her chin on her shoulder and causing a whiff of her favourite floral perfume to infuse the air.

'Oh, it's okay! Everyone's still here. Look, there's Freddie and Matt.'

Rosie swung her gaze around the makeshift camp where everyone was still asleep in exactly the same places they'd chosen to bed down for the night. But her smile of relief quickly disappeared as she realized what that meant.

'Wait a minute - that means we've *all* missed the show! How could Matt have allowed that to happen? Quick!'

With Mia close behind, she scampered out from the tent and shook Matt's shoulder. 'Matt! Matt! Wake up!'

'Ergh?'

'We've missed sunrise!'

'What?' Matt dragged his body into a sitting position, rubbing his broad palm over his chin as he struggled to focus his eyes on Rosie. 'What time is it?'

'Ten past seven. We've missed sunrise but we can still hike up to the priory.'

Everyone in the camp was beginning to stir, woken by the noise.

'What's going on?' called Phil, shaking his head and screwing up his eyes. 'Oh my God, have we slept in? How on earth did that happen?'

'I'm not sure,' replied Matt, his forehead creased into lines of concern. 'My watch alarm definitely isn't broken and there is no way I would have slept through it.'

'Don't worry, Matt. It can happen to the best of us. So, what's the plan?' asked Phil, pointing his camera at the horizon to take a few snaps of the rising sun as it sent fissures of apricot light over the surrounding countryside. 'I'd still like to visit the priory and get some photographs for the book.'

A giggle rippled through the air causing everyone to turn their heads to where Brad and Emma were engaged in what Rosie could only describe as a vigorous tickle fight. She averted her eyes, embarrassed at the intimate scene.

'Hey, you two. You need to get ready. We leave in five minutes!' Matt's voice held a note of steel as he strode away from the gathering, his jaw set and eyes narrowed as he started to dismantle the tent. Freddie collected the rest of the equipment together, stuffed it in his rucksack and took a slug from his water bottle, confusion written across his face.

'Hey, wait a minute! Where's Rick?' called Phil, switching his eyes from left to right as he scoured the camp for his tormentor. 'He's missing.'

'What?' exclaimed Matt, Freddie and Mia in unison.

Rosie scoured the camp site and it was true. There was no sign of Rick or his possessions, just an indentation in the grass where he'd presumably rested for the night. She, and the rest of the expedition members, immediately understood what had happened.

'He's sneaked off without us!' cried Phil, his voice all a-bluster. 'He wanted to be the only one to witness the sunrise through the arch so he could crow about it at our Myth Seekers meetings for all eternity. Oh God, Brad, we should have realized he'd plan something like this. Selfish to the core is our Mr Richard Forster. Right! He's not going to get away with it this time. I've had enough of his...'

Phil patted the pockets of his utility jacket, searching for his mobile phone. Pushing his glasses up onto his forehead, he squinted at the screen and selected Rick's number, then waited for his adversary to answer.

'Either he's ignoring us or there's no signal over by the priory. Wait until I get my hands on...'

'Okay, okay,' announced Matt, clearly struggling to keep his temper under wraps. 'We stick together, all right? No one goes ahead and no one lags behind.'

Matt and Freddie strode away from the campsite leaving the rest of the group to scamper after them. Rosie could feel the anger radiating from Matt's pores and she didn't blame him in the slightest. He had taken personal responsibility for their expedition, given the landowner his word they would stick together and keep to the previously authorized route. She just hoped that Rick hadn't done anything else to jeopardize the reputation of Ultimate Adventures. Willerby was a tight-knit community built on trust and mutual respect and she knew Matt and Freddie would be fuming at Rick's selfish behaviour.

Rosie slipped her arm through Mia's and together they stumbled along the flint-strewn pathway, their bafflement as to the reasons behind Rick's solo excursion keeping their tongues still and their brains occupied.

Why would Rick do such a thing?

It wasn't difficult to come up with the answer. Since he and Helen had checked into their luxury lodges the previous day, Rick Forster had certainly not gone out of his way to endear himself to anyone, wearing his competitive streak like a badge of honour on his chest for all to see. Leaving everyone behind was typical behaviour that perhaps either Phil or Brad, or even Emma, should have anticipated; they were in the Myth Seekers Society with him, after all.

However, what Rosie couldn't understand was how they had all slept beyond Matt's alarm call, except for Rick. Her head was clear now but she couldn't ignore the woolly feeling she'd experienced when she had woken up, and wondered fleetingly if Rick could have put something in their night-time coffee. The thought sent a donkey's kick of shock reverberating through her chest. Yes! That was exactly what had happened! How dare he! She had to talk to Matt immediately.

Rosie jogged to where Matt was leading the group, his head bent low, his eyes narrowed as he concentrated on the task in hand to prevent himself from exploding with exasperation at Rick's selfish tactics in a bout of one-upmanship. Freddie offered her a weak smile and, with a look of relief, dropped back to continue the trek with Mia.

'Matt?'

'Mmm?'

Rosie swallowed down on the anger that had started to bubble in her stomach. If what she suspected was right, the ramifications went far beyond a harmless caper to ensure a personal ring-side seat at a mystical sunrise – spiking some-one's drink with a sleeping drug was nothing short of criminal behaviour! It was outrageous!

'I don't know about you, but when I woke up this morning my head felt like it had been stuffed with cotton wool. Mia said she thought she had a hangover, but not a drop of alcohol passed our lips last night, I promise you. I think, well ... I think Rick might have put something in our coffee last night just so he could experience the sunrise alone.'

'That's exactly the conclusion I've come to. It's simply not possible that both Freddie and I slept through the alarm without some sort of chemical assistance, and you're right, the most likely culprit is Rick. It's exactly the sort of juvenile prank he would find hilarious and another way of belittling the other members of the group. I want to say that we should wait until we speak to him, to give him the benefit of the doubt before making accusations, but I'm so angry that I'm looking at my common sense in the rear-view window!'

'Do you think we should call the police?'

'I do, but not before I've had the chance to give him a piece of my mind. I think we should keep our suspicions to ourselves for the time being though, because when Freddie finds out what Rick's done, it'll be a bit more than a piece of his mind he'll be sending his way. This sort of reckless behaviour is what ruins businesses like Ultimate Adventures. If any of our clients hear even a whiff of the word "drugs" they'll steer well clear. I could strangle him!'

Rosie saw the corners of Matt's mouth tighten as he reigned in his fury, and after a few seconds it was replaced with a glint of his habitual mischief.

'There's one positive though.'

'What's that?' she asked, her stomach performing a back-flip at the way Matt was looking at her from beneath his long, spidery eyelashes. She knew they were both wary of embarking on new relationships because of their recent histories, but she enjoyed the familiar pull of attraction that was often close to the surface whenever she was in his company, breathing in the delicious lemony cologne he favoured. Some people just seemed to occupy the same wavelength, and so it seemed to be with her and Matt.

'At least this time no one was poisoned!'

'Thank God! What do you think Rick put in our coffee?'

'It had to be some kind of sleeping tablets, but we'll leave that to the professionals to work out. Or were you thinking of undertaking the investigation yourself like last time?'

'Well, we did make a great team ... and we got results!'

'You know, Rosie, before you arrived in Willerby, life chugged along quite nicely. The most excitement to be had in the village was a flight down the zip wire or a stint on the obstacle course after a downpour. But now you're in our midst we're dealing with poisoned pop stars and morons who think they can go around lacing people's coffee!'

'Are you saying I attract trouble?'

'No, I...'

'Look! There's the Garside Priory!' cried Phil excitedly, elbowing Rosie and Matt out of the way and increasing his speed to a canter.

'Keep to the path,' shouted Matt, grabbing onto the back of Phil's jacket to prevent him from dashing ahead.

Rosie's calf muscles screamed their objection to the vigorous early morning workout, but a curl of excitement mingled with her irritation over the potential fallout of Rick's irresponsible stunt when the priory appeared in the next field. Even though it was almost a ruin, made up of crumbling stone stitched together by ribbons of ivy, the building still held a mysterious presence. She felt privileged to be there, despite missing the spectacle of the sun rising through the arched doorway.

They had arrived at the wooden gate blocking their access to the site and paused to allow Brad and Emma, now bringing up the rear, to catch up with them. Brad's arm was casually slung around Emma's slender shoulders and he was trying to kiss her. She laughed, pushed him away, and ran towards them, her short auburn hair flapping in the breeze like she was the star in a shampoo advert.

'I can't see Rick anywhere,' said Mia, standing on her tiptoes to look over the yew hedge.

'I reckon he's hiding behind one of the walls, waiting to leap out and startle us. It's the sort of thing he'd do,' said Phil, curling his lip in disgust as he lined up his camera for another shot. 'And I wouldn't put it past him to be dressed in some sort of warlock outfit with false blood dripping from a cere-monial dagger. Rosie, Mia, you have been warned.'

'If he has any sense he'll be running for his life!' retorted Freddie. 'I could kill him.'

'Me too,' muttered Matt as he lifted the iron bar on the gate to allow them to enter the grounds together. He carefully refastened the gate behind them and led them along a narrow footpath towards the priory, pausing at the entrance. 'Okay, so despite having missed the sunrise, I'm sure you'll all still be able to enjoy the experience of being in such a fascinating place. Feel free to explore and we'll meet back here in an hour.'

'Thanks, Matt,' smiled Emma, fluttering her eyelashes ever

so slightly at him before disappearing off to explore with Brad in tow.

Rosie chose to join Matt and Phil as they strode purposefully toward the centre of the fabled stone archway so she could make a wish. Mia had already confided in her that she intended to send up a prayer to the medieval gods that the Windmill Café's autumn party went without a hitch so that Graham would give them more freedom and more cash to spend on their Christmas festivities for which Mia had planned an ambitious tree-decoration competition.

'What are you going to do about Rick?' asked Freddie, whilst they all stood watching Mia caress the stones as she listened intently to Phil's running commentary before disappearing off with him to look at another pile of ancient architecture.

'I'm going to wait until I've calmed down a bit before I decide. What he's done is way out of order, Fred. This isn't some children's adventure quest or treasure hunt. It wasn't easy getting Giles Barringer to agree to a group of myth seeking enthusiasts invading his land for a session of wild camping.'

'Well, there's no lasting harm done, I suppose,' mused Freddie, clearly oblivious to Matt and Rosie's suspicions. 'Except to his relationship with Phil and Brad who are devastated to have missed the main event – I don't think Emma minds all that much, though. I don't know how they put up with his obnoxious arrogance and ridiculous pursuit of one-upmanship, or why. He's a total moron, if you ask me!'

'Well, it's probably because he paid for everyone's trip to

Willerby, including this wild camping jaunt with Ultimate Adventures, out of his own pocket,' said Rosie, making her way down to the arch. No point coming all this way and not taking advantage of the wish-granting facilities. Goodness knew she could do with a bit of help!

'Pardon?'

Matt stared at Rosie, his proximity sending tiny shivers down her spine. Memories of the kiss they'd shared on a deserted Norfolk beach flickered across her mind and caused her to run the tip of her tongue along her lower lip before continuing. 'Rick paid for the lodges; for him and Helen, for Phil and Steph, and for Brad and Emma.'

'But I thought the trip was arranged through the Myth Seekers Society that they all belong to? Like a sort of school trip?'

'It was. But the lodges are expensive, Matt. Graham told me that Rick was so keen to come here to see the Garside Priory that he paid for the majority of the cost without running the real amount past the committee in case they kicked up a fuss about his choice of accommodation. Surprisingly enough, the members are sticklers for the rules. The Society could never have afforded the rental, and neither could Phil or Brad, I suspect. Rick asked Graham not to divulge the fact he'd paid for everything, or how much the lodges actually cost – the others just think the fees were cheap enough that the Society's funds could cover it all.'

'It's certainly a generous gesture, I suppose. But if you want my opinion it's yet another example of his controlling personality. Why couldn't he have come down to Norfolk by himself, or with his wife? Why does he have to have the others with him? Do you think it's just so that he can bounce his superiority and rudeness around unchecked?'

'Probably,' laughed Rosie.

'Arrrrrrrrrrrr!'

A high-pitched scream sliced through the air and Rosie knew at once it was Mia. Her first thought was that she had fallen from a wall, or tumbled into a hollow filled with spiders. She dashed into the middle of the priory's internal courtyard with Matt and Freddie hot on her heels, but what she saw was so unexpected that she drew up short causing Matt to run into the back of her.

She had been right, it was Mia who had screamed – but it wasn't Mia who was injured. Her friend was staring, her hands covering her mouth in horror, at a body slumped on the ground with an arrow protruding from its ankle and blood oozing from the wound.

'Oh my God! It's Rick!'

Chapter 5

Rosie's heart raced in a futile attempt to escape its cage and its thunderous beat rang in her ears. A surge of nausea ambushed her as she turned away from the scene and arched her back to the sky, her palms on her thighs, inhaling ragged gasps of oxygen. She waited for the dizziness to pass. The urge to collapse to her knees was almost too overwhelming to resist but she knew she needed to stay strong for Mia's sake. She swallowed down on the acidic tang radiating over her tongue and with great difficulty managed to drag her senses into some sort of order, hoping for comprehension to dawn.

'Is he ... is he dead?' whimpered Mia.

Phil was next to join them, and the shock of seeing Rick collapsed on the ground in the cloister with Matt kneeling over him and clearly checking for a pulse, rendered him motionless. His jaw gaped, his face bleached chalk white, as he struggled to understand what his eyes were telling him.

'He's not dead, Mia, he's just passed out,' said Matt, grabbing his first aid kit from his rucksack and signalling for Freddie to help him to remove the arrow protruding from Rick's ankle.

'I feel awful saying this, but are you sure he's unconscious?' said Phil, a catch in his throat as he spoke for the first time. 'You've seen what he's like. This could be just another one of his pranks — a joke arrow, fake blood, you know. Sorry, no, forget I said that, sorry.'

Phil took a quick step back and bumped into Brad, who had just arrived on the scene with a breathless Emma in his wake.

'What's going on? Mia, why were you screaming? Oh, my God, what's happened to Rick?'

Shock spread across Emma's face. She folded her arms across her abdomen and huddled against Brad. Her eyes, the colour of Irish shamrock, were as wide as saucers, their whites almost popping from her skull.

Before anyone could answer Emma's questions, Rick started to groan. Rosie had never heard such a welcome complaint. Like Mia, she too had been convinced Rick was dead. Relief flooded her veins and the high-pitched drumming in her ears began to subside. She took a few steadying breaths and as the initial shock eased, her heartbeat returned to something approaching normal. She moved forward to hook her arm around her friend's waist, distressed to feel her uncontrollable trembling.

'Ergh! Careful!'

Beads of perspiration appeared on Rick's forehead and his face displayed a strange waxy pallor. Matt worked quickly to clean Rick's wound and wrap his ankle tightly in a bandage, causing his patient to grimace as spasms of pain shot through his calf with each twist.

'Can you remember anything about what happened?' asked Matt, sitting back on his heels, satisfied he had done the best he could in the circumstances.

'What does it look like? Someone shot me with an arrow! Their first attempt went flying past my ear and got stuck in that bench over there. I tried to run, but they got me with their second shot. I reckon if I hadn't collapsed behind that gravestone, they would have finished the job, or maybe they just chickened out, I don't know. Anyway, I must have passed out from the pain, because the next thing I know you're yanking the bloody thing from my ankle. Is it broken?'

'I think it's just a flesh wound, in which case there'll be no lasting damage, but it's probably best to get your ankle checked out at hospital. I'll call an ambulance...'

'There's no mobile signal,' interrupted Freddie, his freckled face suffused in anxiety. 'It's half a mile to the nearest village. I'll run over there and call the paramedics and then wait for them at the end of the track to guide them up here to the priory.'

'Thanks, Freddie.'

'I don't need an ambulance, I want the police!'

'So you don't think it was an accident?' gasped Mia, her tone raised an octave in alarm.

'Of course not! Who accidentally fires off *two* arrows in the same direction? And do you see anyone hanging around to apologize for their seriously substandard archery skills? No, you don't. Which can only mean one thing – I was targeted by a lunatic intent on dispatching me to my maker in broad daylight.'

'But who would...? Oh my God! Do you think the person who did this is still ... is still...?'

Rosie's voice trailed off into the enveloping silence as everyone, apart from Rick, turned in unison to scan the crumbling eaves of the priory, then the copse of trees to their left, then finally to watch Freddie's retreating figure as he made his way across the field towards civilization, all of them expecting him to collapse under a barrage of arrows at any moment.

'Did anyone see anything on the hike over here? Anything at all?' asked Matt.

'Well, I didn't see anything, or any*one* escaping over the fields in green tights carrying a quiver full of arrows,' said Brad, the only one seemingly unmoved by Rick's suffering and subsequent hypothesis of being a victim in a pre-meditated shooting.

'Well, it's obvious who the culprit is, isn't it?' seethed Rick.

'Who?' demanded Rosie.

'Well, no one else knew we were going to be here, did they? It's highly unlikely that a passer-by, who just happened to be carrying a bow and arrow in their back pocket, decided to take aim and shoot a random stranger who was innocently exploring an ancient priory at dawn.'

'Does that mean...'

'Rick, you can't seriously be suggesting that one of us is responsible for shooting you.'

'No other explanation.'

'You are unbelievable!' muttered Brad, his eyes reflecting his contempt for Rick's theory. 'Someone correct me if I'm wrong, but haven't we all been together from the moment we left camp until Mia discovered Rick slumped here in the cloisters? How could any one of us have shot you with a bow and arrow?'

'Brad does have a point,' said Phil, his hands shaking so violently on his camera that he was forced to shove them into the pockets of his combat trousers, but his elbows continued to flap nervously at his sides like a caged seagull.

'Okay,' interrupted Matt, keen to diffuse the mounting tension. 'This is neither the time, nor the place, to be making unfounded accusations. Phil, would you mind taking Emma and Mia back to the reception lodge at Ultimate Adventures? Brad, I need you to stay to help carry Rick's stretcher to the ambulance. Rosie, I take it you've got first aid training, so can you stay here too, until Freddie gets back with the paramedics?'

'And the police! I think everyone should stay where they are, not go wandering off! We need to find out who tried to kill me, and why, as soon as possible so they can feel the full strength of the law!'

'But why would any one of us want to kill you, Rick? And why here in Norfolk? We've all had ample opportunity to bump you off back home in Manchester,' reasoned Brad, glancing around the gathering to make sure everyone was agreeing with him.

'Hey, maybe it was one of the ghosts or spirits who inhabit the ruin?' suggested Emma, speaking for the first time since they had found Rick collapsed in a pool of blood.

'You know, I've changed my mind. Matt's right, you should

head back. I don't want to sit here, forced to listen to such ridiculous hypotheses for the next hour. All I ask is that when you eventually manage get back to civilization, one of you informs Helen so she can drive over to the hospital to collect me – if she isn't too busy spending my money in the shops of Norwich. Think you can manage that, Phil?'

'Of course. Come on, ladies, let's get going.'

'And make sure you stick to the path,' advised Matt, repacking the Ultimate Adventures first aid box and returning it to his rucksack.

'Yeah, and try not to get an arrow between your eyes,' warned Rick, with more than a soupçon of malice in his expression.

'What if Rick's right and there *is* someone lurking out there?' said Emma, her anguish plain for all to see. 'A poison-tipped arrow could be trained on any one of us at this very moment. I could be the next victim! Oh God!'

'Don't worry,' said Phil, patting Emma's arm awkwardly. 'I think whoever did this will be long gone by now, and once we get under cover of those trees over there, I reckon we'll be safe. Best we do as Matt says and stay close, though.'

Emma nodded mutely, reached up to deposit a quick kiss on Brad's lips and then linked Mia's arm with hers. Together, the threesome made their way back along the pathway across the field, at the end of which Phil took great care to refasten the wooden gate behind him. Brad stared after them, a touch of envy in his expression, his broad shoulders sunken under the weight of the ongoing trauma.

'I'll just go and see if there's any sign of that ambulance,' announced Matt, scrambling to his feet. 'Could you sit with Rick until I get back, please, Brad?'

'Oh, I ... yes, okay.'

'I'll come with you,' offered Rosie when she caught sight of the anguish and confusion on Matt's face.

A spasm of sympathy rushed through her chest. She was sure that the very last thing he would have expected to deal with during an early morning hike to the Garside Priory was one of his charges being shot by a stray arrow. Only Rick appeared to be suggesting that it was no accident and that someone had targeted him. As she followed Matt through the mystical archway, her whole body froze when another, more sinister thought occurred to her. Did Rick's shooting have anything to do with the fact that she and Matt suspected something had been added to their evening coffee? And if so, what did it mean? Who could...

She was prevented from chasing that terrifying scenario down blind alleyways by the sharp indignant barks of a young black-and-white Collie who had rushed up to greet them. The Collie's owner, a man in his late fifties wearing a well-worn wax jacket straining over his well-padded stomach, issued a whistled warning and the dog returned to heel.

'Grim business,' the man grunted, a tight expression stretching his weathered face as he inclined his head towards the priory while holding out his hand for Matt to shake. Seeing their astonished expressions, he continued, 'Freddie Armstrong just called to ask me to open the bottom gate so the ambulance can get through.'

'Rosie, this is Giles Barringer, he owns the land around the priory.'

'Pleased to meet you, Giles.'

'So, who is the guy?'

'Richard Forster – chairman of the Myth Seekers Society I told you about,' explained Matt, bending down to fondle the dog's silky ears. 'Found him collapsed in the central cloister with an arrow through his leg. Better be careful, we're not sure whether the perpetrator is still in the area.'

'Right you are,' said the farmer as though that sort of thing happened all the time. He eyed Matt for a few moments before he spoke again. 'Well, no one came by the farm – that I can guarantee you. Our Bess here, and her sister Meggie, go mental whenever strangers breach their radar. Reckon whoever it was must have come up via your overnight camp.'

'Thanks, Giles. I'll keep you informed.'

They bade the farmer farewell and strolled back towards the cloister in silence, each subsumed by a swirl of unpleasant thoughts and theories as to what might have happened.

'Are you going to confront Rick about putting a sedative in our coffee?'

'Actually, after what's just happened, I think I might have been a bit quick to jump to conclusions.'

'So you think the two things are connected?'

'Possibly. But you're right, we do need to ask Rick about it.'

When they arrived, Brad was slumped against his rucksack, his knees drawn into his chest, keeping a close eye on Rick who had passed out again.

'Why would anyone want to shoot Rick?' mused Rosie, almost to herself, as she sat down next to Brad.

'Well...' began Brad, tossing a quick glance over his shoulder to make sure Rick definitely hadn't woken up. He fiddled nervously with the zipper of his Gore-Tex running jacket, a vein working overtime at his temple.

'If you know something, Brad, you have to tell us,' snapped Matt, sitting up straighter and fixing him with a stern stare. 'This is a very serious situation; one which could have a devastating effect, not only on my business, but on Freddie and Mia's futures, too, if we don't get to the bottom of what happened quickly. We can't just brush this under the carpet and file it away under a heading marked "accident". The police are going to be involved, they will want to investigate what happened, and even if it turns out to be an organized field archery expedition that went seriously wrong, visitors to the area might think twice about booking an outward-bound activity – especially if there's an outside chance of getting shot with a stray arrow, don't you think? This is mine and Rosie's livelihoods at stake!'

'So, you really think the police will want to question us?'

Rosie heard the catch in Brad's voice when he said the word 'police'. However, she stored it away for future dissection when she saw the familiar gleam in Matt's eyes as he gave her a surreptitious nod. She knew exactly what he was thinking. If they could persuade Brad to open up about the Myth Seekers Society, maybe they could work together to uncover the truth surrounding Rick's injury – just as they had in August with Suki Richards' poisoning – before the consequences destroyed their respective businesses.

What if Rick's injury meant they had to cancel the Autumn Leaves party at the end of the week? Mia would be devastated, not to mention everyone in Willerby who had helped to organize the celebrations and whipped up homemade contributions. After the debacle with Harry in London, she had a lot to be thankful to the community for, and she was prepared to do whatever it took, not only to maintain her happy home in the little circular studio above the Windmill Café, but also to ensure that what had happened to Rick did not reflect badly on the reputation of Ultimate Adventures and that the Willerby residents had a fabulous Hallowe'en party.

'Please, Brad, Matt and I just want to help.'

The thought of teaming up with Matt again to unravel a mystery sent a frisson of excitement cascading through her veins and sparkling out to her fingertips. However, she recognized that the cauldron of emotions whipping through her stomach were not solely connected with the chance to investigate another mystery, but also to do with the way Matt was holding her gaze and the fragrance of his citrusy cologne that tickled at her nostrils.

'Brad?'

'Okay, okay, sorry,' said Brad, running his fingers nervously through his hair. 'Well, I could be way out of line, but here goes. I'm sure you've both noticed that none of us like Rick very much – he's an obnoxious bully and a complete pain in the backside. If someone had given me a quiver full of sharpened arrows, I might have taken a pop at him myself. But, if it wasn't some random stranger, then out of all of us I reckon Phil has the strongest motive for wanting him to suffer.'

'What do you mean?' demanded Rosie, tipping her head back so she could look Brad in the eye, her natural inquisitiveness reasserting its dominance. She could almost feel her father, who had adored mysteries just as much as she did, sending down vibes of encouragement to seek out the truth and slot each new discovery into the overall jigsaw to form a picture of exactly what had happened.

'Well, you saw how Rick went on with Phil last night. He's exactly the same at our meetings. Rick only joined the Myth Seekers Society ten months ago but he made sure he stamped his personality on our little club straight away. We'd plodded along in our own sweet way for years. Phil was our chairman, our treasurer *and* our secretary. No one else wanted the responsibility, or the hassle and paperwork that went with it, but Phil likes that sort of thing. We managed one expedition a year and a couple of local jaunts. It was fun, everyone was a real enthusiast. It was a break from the daily grind to five o'clock, if you know what I mean.'

Brad paused, his Adam's apple bobbing in his throat as he gathered his courage to continue. It was obvious to Rosie that Brad was missing Emma's more forceful presence; his girlfriend might be petite in stature but she made up for it in strength of personality. Nevertheless, he inhaled a deep breath and continued with his story.

'Then Rick arrived on the scene. He organized a formidable schedule of guest speakers – himself included – and sourced videos made by myth seekers from all over the world. He even set up a blog for us all to post our research on. In the beginning, we loved it. We got to learn loads more about myth-seeking, and the trips he arranged were excellent. We went to the Isle of Man in the summer to visit the famous Fairy Bridge and it was Rick's idea to come here to Norfolk so he could continue his research into the local legends, including the one about the Black Shuck. His theory is...'

'Brad, is this relevant?' interrupted Matt, trying hard not to roll his eyes at Rosie.

'Sorry, sorry. What I mean is, the club changed. All of a sudden Phil found himself side-lined. Rick took over as chairman, appointed one of the newer members as secretary and Phil was left in the thankless role of treasurer. Every meeting was an opportunity for Rick to lord it over everyone else – he even gave himself the title of King Myth Seeker. He had polo shirts embroidered with the society's emblem and demanded we all wear them to the meetings. He was a true enthusiast, though. He researched every detail and shared all his findings with us. I loved it, but I've never seen anyone so obsessed with the research and after a while it all started to get too technical.

'In the end I just stuck it out for the subsidized trips. As well as the trip over to the Isle of Man, the group have been to Rome, Marrakesh and Athens in the last twelve months. I'd never be able to afford any of that on my salary. Emma and I are extreme sports enthusiasts too – wild climbing, fell-running, orienteering and we try to run as many marathons as we can – so it all adds up.'

'So, you're saying Phil had his nose pushed out by Rick?' asked Rosie, totally engrossed in the story of the Myth Seekers Society.

'More than that. Rick seemed to have Phil marked as his

personal punch bag – verbal, not physical. For some reason, Rick takes great pleasure in tormenting him every chance he gets. It's embarrassing for all of us when he starts on one of his campaigns of ridicule and derision. I'm ashamed to confess that we don't challenge him as much as we should. We're all just grateful it isn't us, and anyway Rick was paying for the hire of the hall from his own funds as well as other extras. I have tried to call him out a few times, but he'd switch his focus if you weren't careful.'

'A bit cowardly, don't you think?' said Matt, glancing over his shoulder at Rick, an expression of dislike written across his handsome features.

'Yes, I realize that now,' agreed Brad. 'We should have made a stand and voted him off the committee months ago. Rick's scary though, like a big fish in a little pond, or more like a vicious shark who uses his financial muscle to take over and advance his own agenda. Phil might have a really good reason to shoot Rick with an arrow, but he's actually an honest, trustworthy, and thoroughly decent guy who's been treated disgracefully by all of us for not standing up to Rick's intimidation.'

Before either Rosie or Matt could respond to Brad's theory on the identity of Rick's attacker, the man himself had started to groan again and a series of flashing blue lights signalled the arrival of the paramedics. Rosie did what she could to assist in the transportation of Rick's prostate, complaining body on a stretcher across the uneven field before they were all told in no uncertain terms that he did not require a chaperone for the journey to hospital.

With an elongated sigh, she jumped into the back of a Jeep belonging to one of Freddie's bandmates and spent the journey back to Ultimate Adventures with random thoughts ricocheting around her brain as she tried to make sense of what had happened. She was relieved when the jutting roof of the outward-bound centre's reception lodge came into view, but the respite from anxiety lasted only a few seconds.

'Thank God you're back!' said Emma, throwing herself into Brad's arms as they all gathered on the veranda. 'Now, who's going to ring Helen?'

Chapter 6

Rosie drew into the Windmill Café car park, the tyres of her Mini Cooper making a satisfying crunch on the gravel. Every time she heard that sound she sent up a missive to the director of her destiny, sending thanks for guiding her to Willerby. The heartbreak she had endured in the Pimlico flower shop was so firmly in the past now that she felt as though it had happened to someone else.

'Do you think they made the right decision?' asked Mia.

'I think so. I'm sure Helen would much rather hear the news about her husband's accident face-to-face than over the phone. And it's only taken us ten minutes to drive from Ultimate Adventures to the lodges, so there hasn't been much of a delay.'

Rosie leapt out of the passenger's seat and with Mia by her side, jogged to catch up with Phil, Brad and Emma as they made their way towards the field next to the café where the four luxury lodges were situated. Her heart bounced around her chest like an escaped yo-yo as the full force of what had happened hit her – once again misfortune had befallen one of their guests.

Thankfully, this time the cause could not be connected to the Windmill Café, but she wasn't in the slightest tempted to wash her hands of the whole affair. Knowing Rick, he would make as much fuss as possible about the lax security provided by Ultimate Adventures, irrespective of the fact that even the most thorough of risk assessments could not have foreseen the possibility of a client being shot by a stray arrow! Matt and Freddie had been steadfast in their support of her and the café when she'd had to deal with Suki Richards' poisoning during Graham's absence in Barbados, and she was absolutely committed to returning the favour.

'Hi! I didn't expect you back so soon,' called Phil's wife, Steph, waving cheerfully from the veranda of her lodge like a Fifties housewife greeting her husband home from a hard day at the office

Rosie had warmed to Steph straight away. For some reason she reminded her of her mother, probably because of her penchant for belted tea dresses sprinkled with tiny sprigs of flowers, not to mention the iron-set mousey-brown curls which made her look like she was wearing a helmet. While her husband was a fanatic in the fantasy and legend department, it turned out that Steph was an avid follower of all things culinary which had served to seal their instant friendship. When the café had closed its doors to paying customers on Saturday night, Rosie, Mia, Steph and Helen had whipped up a mountain of meringue for an apricot and vanilla pavlova, and Steph had confessed to an addiction to daytime TV cookery shows.

Steph had also spoken enthusiastically about her WI's

cookery demonstrations and bubbled over with child-like excitement at being given the chance to learn a few tips from a couple of professionals. They had enjoyed a wonderful laughter-filled evening baking a batch of coffee-flavoured cupcakes and decorating them with cappuccino frosting topped with crushed walnuts, before devouring their bakes with a bottle of prosecco.

Helen, on the other hand, had been an enthusiast newbie, giggling at the sunken middle of her cakes before declaring that she intended to fill the holes with chocolate buttons and no one would suspect the disaster. After all, as long as it tasted good, what did it matter?

Emma had arrived later and helped to whip up the double cream, adding a generous slug of amaretto liqueur. It had been a relaxing, fun-filled evening of gossip, fizz and confectionery whilst the men had spent their time hunched over old books planning their Sunday afternoon trip to see a witch's leg in a medieval church and prepare for their night of wild camping.

How could such a happy sojourn have been shattered by something so awful?

'Where's Helen, Steph?' asked Phil, glancing over to Rick and Helen's lodge as though it was the dreaded dentist's surgery.

'Oh, she's taken the Porsche for an early spin to the village. She must have pushed a note through my door before I woke up this morning.' Steph swung her pale blue gaze around the disconsolate group. Obviously, it wasn't hard to conclude that something untoward had happened. 'Why isn't Rick with you?'

Rosie exchanged a worried glance with Mia, ashamed to admit how relieved she was that Helen wasn't there, despite the fact that they were simply putting off the inevitable. She wondered if it was possible for Rick to return from the hospital before Helen got back from her shopping trip so they could leave it to him to explain what had happened.

'Why don't we all go over to the café? I'm sure everyone could do with a cup of tea.'

'Great idea,' said Phil, ignoring the look of confusion on Steph's face, hooking his arm through hers and following the group down to the café.

'I'm starving,' announced Brad. 'Do you think you could rustle up some eggs, Rosie?'

'Sure.'

A wave of relief spread through Rosie's chest as she stepped into her beloved Windmill Café. The place was pristine, with everything in its allocated spot and the faintest whiff of Flash lingering in the air that gave her comfort whilst the world crumbled around her – at least her little part of the universe still held some order. She felt the fuzziness in her brain lift and clear, and couldn't wait to get stuck in to her favourite pastime of feeding friends, customers and visitors.

It was Monday morning and the café was closed to customers now until the Autumn Leaves Hallowe'en party on Saturday night. After much consideration, Graham had decreed that the café would only open at weekends from the end of October until March, but the holiday site would remain available to guests who enjoyed the cooler weather and invigorating walks.

With Mia's help, Rosie scrambled around the kitchen gathering the essential ingredients for a light breakfast despite her suspicions that only Brad would manage even a mouthful. She poured out mugs of thick, dark tea for everyone, added a spoonful of sugar to each, then wiped down the oven, sprayed the marble countertops, and checked the cupboards to satisfy herself that they were as tidy as Hercules Poirot's bathroom cabinet. Finally, she took a seat next to Mia on one of the sofas next to the French doors to try to eat a slice of toast and jam.

'What's going on?' asked Steph, her eyes jumping from one person to the next. 'I know something's happened. Has ... has Helen had an accident in the Porsche?' Her hand flew to her lips and tiny creases appeared on her forehead and at the corners of her eyes and mouth. Droplets of tea sloshed from her mug onto her pristine dress.

'No, it's Rick, I'm afraid,' said Phil, taking Steph's bird-like hand in his and turning in his seat to face her. 'He's, erm, he's had an accident at the Garside Priory. We need to contact Helen to tell her...'

'Is he okay?'

'He's fine, darling, just being checked over at the hospital.'

Steph looked across at Brad and Emma who were both hugging their mugs into their chests like comfort blankets, unable to meet Steph's eyes for fear she would ask them to answer her questions. They both looked as if they were ready to keel over – so much for the physical stamina of extreme sports addicts, thought Rosie, but she immediately chastised herself for her unkind thoughts. It must have been a huge shock to see their friend with an arrow protruding from his ankle, even if they didn't like him very much.

'Our friend Freddie who works at Ultimate Adventures called the police, so they'll probably want to ask us a few questions. We'll have to give statements...' began Rosie.

'The police? But why are the police...'

'Will you ring Helen, please, Steph?'

'Yes, yes of course.'

Steph removed her mobile from the pocket of her pale apricot cardigan, stooping forward to retrieve her lace handkerchief that had fallen to the floor. She waited whilst the call rang and then left a voicemail asking Helen to ring either her or Rick urgently.

'Her phone must be switched off.'

'Where did you say Helen's gone?'

'I'm not sure what her note said exactly. I'll go and fetch it, shall I?'

Steph rushed from the café and made her way back to her lodge. As the silence stretched, Rosie walked over to the French windows and lingered on the threshold, taking in the panorama. Above her, the larks and curlews were going about their daily business oblivious to the drama unfolding on the ground below them. To her right, a spiral of grey smoke wove into the electric blue sky from the woodland beyond which lay St Andrew's church and the village of Willerby.

She wondered where Matt was and how he was feeling. From what she knew about Rick, she suspected he would not pass up the opportunity to list Ultimate Adventures' numerous perceived failings in great detail, possibly in writing, probably in triplicate. She wanted to talk to him, to reassure him that she was eager to dust off the metaphorical deerstalker she had inherited from her father and continue with the line of questioning they had started with Brad, not sit around in the café drinking tea whilst they located the whereabouts of Rick's missing wife as she gave her husband's credit card an outing.

When she recalled the way Matt's dark blue eyes had lingered on hers as she and Mia had bedded down for the night, her stomach gave an involuntary lurch. Her feelings for him confused her and now wasn't the time to unravel them, so she shoved them into the crevices of her mind for later dissection. One thing she did know was that she loved being in his company, and had enjoyed solving the mystery of Suki Richards' poisoning before the police had even produced their notebooks – and there was no reason why they couldn't do the same again.

As she watched Steph lock the door of her lodge and canter back down the pathway towards the café, another thought occurred to her. Should she ring Graham to let him know what had happened whilst he was sunning himself on his brother's yacht in Palma? She could just see the look of incredulity on his craggy face as he absorbed the fact that his new café manager had attracted more trouble. It didn't take her long to decide against contacting him. After all, this time the unfortunate incident had happened miles away from the Windmill Café and the holiday lodges, so why should she bother him with the news until she absolutely had to?

'Do you think Rick's accident could have something to do

with the legend he told us about?' asked Phil who had his notebook open on his lap and was scribbling away with a pencil, his lips pursed in concentration.

'Which legend?' asked Steph as she arrived back at the café with Helen's hand-scribbled note.

'The one that says the Garside Priory is cursed and if you sleep within its perimeter you will die or go mad?' Phil tapped his pencil against his lips as he considered the possibility.

Rosie recalled the myth Rick had told them about – and noticed that Phil had conveniently left out the bit about the intruder becoming a poet.

'He was shot with an arrow! How can a legend be responsible for that?' scoffed Mia, striding to the marble unit to replenish her coffee.

'Ancient myths have to be respected, Mia,' muttered Phil, burying his nose into one of the many dog-eared guidebooks he'd removed from his rucksack and set on the floor at his feet alongside his trusty camera. 'There are loads of myths and legends that originate in and around East Anglia. Perhaps Rick fell foul of the curse about removing one of the stones?'

'But he didn't, did he? He didn't remove anything,' said Mia, her eyes seeking out Rosie for confirmation.

Phil ignored her and continued to study his book, clearly on a roll. 'And there's something in here about that black dog with piercing red eyes who roams the coast and countryside on stormy nights preying on the unsuspecting traveller.'

'And he wasn't savaged to death by a rabid dog, either!' added Emma. 'Next you'll be having us believe that the Brown Lady was the perpetrator!'

'Who's the Brown Lady?' asked Rosie, her interest piqued until she caught Steph's sigh of resignation and immediately regretted her enquiry.

'Oh, it's some ridiculous ghost story Rick forced us to listen to at one of our Myth Seekers meetings before we came down here.' Emma rolled her eyes in mute exasperation. 'We had to sit through a two-hour lecture on local folklore before we were even allowed to put our names down to come on the trip.'

'It was fascinating, I thought,' Phil mused.

'Maybe if you like sitting in a wooden shed freezing your bollocks off all night listening to our Lord and Master drone on about ... sorry ... sorry, Steph,' muttered Brad.

'Rick has his faults, I concede,' said Phil. 'But he's fantastic at uncovering the most obscure stories. He's meticulous in his research and a great public speaker. The Brown Lady of Raynham Hall, Rosie, is one of the most famous ghost photographs in the world, captured by two photographers for *Country Life* magazine in the Thirties. The subject is thought to be Lady Dorothy Townsend who was reportedly locked up in the attic of the hall by her husband which is why she's still wandering the corridors and staircases today.'

'Are you seriously expecting us to believe that the Brown Lady shot Rick in the leg with an arrow? Why? Had he invaded her boudoir?' giggled Emma.

'No, I'm just saying...'

A flash of sunlight glanced through the French doors. Rosie stepped onto the terrace and sucked in a rejuvenating breath of fresh air. Despite it being the end of October, the day promised warmth, but, of course, the elements took no pity on whatever drama was being playing out down below. A maelstrom of anxiety had started to flood her veins.

Where was Helen and why hadn't she called?

Then something else occurred to her. Just because Helen and Steph hadn't accompanied them on the wild camping trek didn't mean they could be omitted from their list of suspects. How easy would it have been for either of them to slip away from their respective lodges under the cover of darkness, drive over to the priory, and wait for an opportunity to fire off an arrow?

Was that why Helen was conspicuous by her absence? Was she really just shopping in Willerby or had she panicked when her second shot had failed to strike the necessary blow and used Rick's Porsche to make a quick getaway?

She wanted to call Matt straight away to ask him what he thought. After all, if the archer's intention had been to murder Rick, wasn't the most likely suspect the victim's wife?

Chapter 7

Rosie made a decision. If she stayed at the café any longer she would continue to concoct ever complicated and elaborate theories that bore no resemblance to the facts. She had to do something practical or she would be looking at her sanity in the rear-view mirror. Instead of spending her time convicting Helen of a crime simply because she had the misfortune to be married to Rick, she should at least try to find her and the best place to start was the village.

'Mia, can you hold the fort here whilst I drive over to Willerby to see if I can find Helen? You know what the village grapevine is like – it'll be humming with the news of the shooting already. I'd hate for her to find out about Rick's accident from a passing stranger.'

'Rosie, are you sure you want to...'

'I'll just have a drive around. It can't be difficult to spot a bright red Porsche, can it?'

'Well, no, but...'

Before Mia could formulate a persuasive argument to the contrary, Rosie ran up the stairs to her flat, grabbed a wax jacket and strode out to the car park. The aroma of wood smoke loitered in the air and the birds continued with their symphony of joy, oblivious to the disturbances on the ground below their perches. She inserted the key into the ignition of her Mini Cooper and crawled through the rose-coloured pebbles down the driveway towards the road that led to Willerby, speeding up when she had the village in her sights.

As she reached the kissing gate of St Andrew's church, a sudden blast of doubt reverberated around her brain. What was she doing? What were the chances of bumping into Helen blithely walking along the high street, with not a care in the world, blissfully unaware that her husband has narrowly escaped an assignation attempt by bow and arrow? She realized that she had used the idea of searching for her as an excuse to escape the atmosphere at the café and immediately a spasm of guilt shot through her body. She shouldn't have left Mia by herself.

It was a few seconds before she realized her phone was vibrating against her leg and she swung into the car park of the Drunken Duck to take the call. She smiled when she saw the caller ID and wasn't in the least bit surprised when Matt offered to joined her at the pub.

'I'm going crazy just sitting here waiting for the police to arrive to question me. They've got my number if they want to speak to me. I've tried several times to speak to Rick, but either his battery has died or he's avoiding my calls. Why don't you get the drinks in and I'll see you in the snug in ten minutes? Mine's a pint of Wherry.'

Rosie chose a corner table and sipped her tonic water. She had considered ordering a glass of her favourite Chianti, but she needed all her little grey cells to be in peak condition if she was going to have any chance of persuading Matt that her theory about Helen being the person responsible was valid. She wondered who was top of his leader board of suspects. Would he agree with Brad and opt for Phil as the most likely candidate? Or, maybe Brad was so keen to point the finger at Phil because he had something to hide himself.

However, before she moved on to consider Emma as a potential suspect she realized there was a flaw in her deliberations. How could Phil, Brad or Emma be the errant archer when they had been in clear sight from the moment they had left camp that morning? This fact gave even more weight to her argument that it could be Helen ... or even Steph. Hadn't Brad said she was like a Rottweiler protecting her brood, or words to that effect. Perhaps she'd endured enough of Rick belittling her husband and decided to take matters into her own hands.

'Hi! God, do I need this!'

Matt plopped himself down next to Rosie and took a long draught of his beer, running the tip of his tongue along his lower lip as if he'd just partaken of the nectar of the gods. Rosie noticed that parallel lines had appeared at his forehead and there were smudges of tiredness beneath his eyes, but they still held that sparkle that caused her heart to quicken.

'Okay, spill.'

'What do you mean?'

'I recognize that look on your face from last time we were sitting in here going through the possible suspects for the poisoning at the Windmill Café. I can tell you're bursting to explain your theory. I don't mind confessing that I'm desperate to find out who did this. I'm worried about the financial impact all this will have on the business, but I'm more concerned about the impact of a potential health and safety scandal on Dad's memory.'

Rosie's heart performed a flip-flop of sympathy when she saw the ragged distress reflected in Matt's eyes and it was apparent he still felt his father's absence deeply.

'What if Ultimate Adventures is closed down, Rosie? I can't have Dad's name dragged through the mud. He's still revered by the climbing community; there's dozens of blogs and vlogs dedicated to his climbing expeditions with thousands of followers. There's even a website where fans can post their own attempts at following in his footsteps. He loved the outward-bound centre, it's his legacy to the climbing community. We still get people booking activities just so they can say they've walked in his shoes, for God's sake.'

Rosie reached across the table and squeezed Matt's hand. She knew the story of Matt's father, Malcolm Wilson; how he'd managed to cram more into his forty-eight years than a normal person managed in one lifetime. He'd completed the Three Peaks challenge, cycled the Coast-to-Coast and hiked the Pennine Way, but the thing he had loved the most was rock climbing; Snowdonia, the Lake District, the Scottish Highlands, the Pyrenees, the Alps. Matt had described his father's hobby as a kind of obsession, as though the mountain in front of him was a vengeful monster barring his way and he couldn't rest until he'd tamed it.

However, there had been one monster he couldn't tame –

the Eiger. He had known the dangers, but had insisted on tackling it anyway. There was a reason it was called The Murder Wall – everyone in his climbing party had perished after a heavy rockfall wiped them from its surface. Matt had been twenty-one when the accident happened, about to start his training in the Police Force which he'd had to abandon to take up the reins at Ultimate Adventures. That was ten years ago and he had told Rosie on several occasions that his father had been right; he would have hated being cooped up in an office, filling in paperwork, battling with bureaucracy and struggling with the networking that was required to climb the career ladder.

'Okay, in that case we'd better get on with investigating what happened to Rick ourselves, speak to everyone who was on the wild camping trek, but I think we should also include those who weren't.'

'Why?'

In as few words as possible, Rosie explained her theory about Helen; how she thought it was odd that on the morning her husband was shot she was absent from her lodge and no one knew for certain where she was, and that her mobile was switched off so they couldn't contact her.

'Actually, that's why I'm here,' Rosie added. 'I told everyone that I'd take a drive around Willerby, ask a few questions to see if anyone has noticed her around this morning. It's can't be difficult to spot her in a bright red Porsche, can it?'

'So, Helen is on your lists of suspects? Is Steph, too?'

'Yes, although she occupies the bottom rung. I just can't see her skipping across the fields in her flowery tea dress with a bow slung over her shoulder and a quiver full of arrows hung around her waist, can you?'

'What, and you can see Helen doing that?'

'You haven't met her. Okay, she's polished, elegant, has fabulous nails, and her outfits cost more than my monthly salary, but she's a gym and yoga fanatic. I don't think she would have any problem at all sprinting from the road to the priory, waiting until Rick came into view and firing off an arrow.'

'Do they offer archery courses at the gyms in Manchester?' smiled Matt, his earlier despondency vanishing as he listened carefully to Rosie's theories.

'I have no idea, but all I'm saying is we shouldn't rule her out. We saw for ourselves how derogatory Rick was to everyone – no one escaped his sarcasm. It wasn't just idle banter either, some of the things he said to his fellow society members really hurt. So, if this is what he's like with them, I've no doubt he's difficult to live with too.'

'So Helen decided to kill him?'

'Well, maybe she just wanted to teach him a lesson? Or to incapacitate him for a while so she could enjoy a peaceful break in the Norfolk countryside. In fact, if I was married to Rick, I would certainly have considered something similar. There's just something about him that tickles at the hackles on the back of my neck.'

'Okay, I agree we need to speak to everyone in the Myth Seekers party. We've already got Brad's take on things. We know he thinks Phil is the most likely candidate, but we need to hear Phil's side of the story too. Maybe he'll be just as eloquent in his suspicions about Brad – and if you want my opinion, he's my number one suspect at the moment. If you're bringing intuition into this, then mine is screaming Brad's name. And what about Emma? Why don't we go back to the Windmill Café and start asking questions?'

'Okay, but before we go, can we just take a quick detour around the village to see if we bump into Helen? I'd feel awful if I went back without even having a look.'

On their way towards the front door of the Drunken Duck, Matt was stopped three times and asked for the details about the shooting of one of the outward-bound visitors. Rosie experienced a sharp stab of sympathy for Matt's predicament which gave her even more incentive to discover how the incident had taken place without any of them seeing anything, who was responsible, and why. It was a tall order, but they had been successful before, so there was no reason why they couldn't do it again.

She smiled at her newfound positivity and self-belief that had emerged from the ashes of her relationship with Harry – which entailed not just the impact of his infidelity but of his constant denigration of her skills as a florist when she had worked with him in their flower shop in Pimlico. There was only one person to thank for the speed of that recovery and he was at her side as they walked past the Post Office and St Andrew's church on their way towards Adriano's Deli. She opened her mouth, about to thank Matt for being a part of her life, when he came to a standstill and grasped her arm.

'Look!'

Rosie scrutinized the stone-fronted houses on a quiet residential side street behind the Post Office, holiday homes most of them, slumbering peacefully as they waited for their absent owners to descend and breathe fresh life into them. One of the properties had been turned into a B&B and she wondered why Matt was so keen to point it out. She turned her head over her shoulder, a question forming on her lips until she saw what he was pointing at.

'Oh my God! That's Helen's Porsche!'

Without waiting for Matt, she sprinted down the path to the car and peered in the window, not sure what she was expecting to see. Helen slumped over the steering wheel with an arrow protruding from her back was one of the images that floated across her mind, swiftly followed by the tip of an arrow pointing between her own eyes. Of course, the Porsche was empty and she heaved a silent sigh of relief.

'Okay, so it looks like she *is* shopping in Willerby, just like she told Steph,' said Matt, turning to make his way back to the main street. 'Come on, we need to find her so she can get across to the hospital as soon as possible. I'm sure Rick will be wondering why she hasn't arrived, or why she hasn't even called him yet.'

'Hang on.'

Rosie paused at the rust-blistered, wrought-iron gate of the B&B, then raised her eyes to the cheerful sunflower-yellow front door, a twist of an idea weaving through her brain. She knew it was left-of-field, but from all the hours she had spent solving fictional murder mysteries in books and at staged parties, she wanted to give her new theory an airing – just like she had with her father before he died.

'What's wrong?'

'Okay, I know this is going to sound crazy, but hear me out. So, perhaps Helen didn't drive over to Garside Priory to shoot Rick this morning, but that doesn't mean she isn't involved in her husband's shooting in some other way, does it? Maybe ... she's visiting someone who was!'

'You're saying you think she had an accomplice?'

'Yes, and that he or she is staying in the B&B and that Helen's inside there now, listening to all the gory details and handing over an envelope of cash.'

It was testament to Matt's friendship, and his respect for her, that he didn't discard her new theory, or indeed laugh in her face with abject incredulity. She could just envisage what Harry would have said if she'd allowed her love of detective stories to formulate such a ridiculous hypothesis.

'Well, Miss Marple, there's only one way to find out!'

Before she knew what was happening, Matt had grabbed her arm and pushed her through the gate. She picked her way over the garden borders, careful not to crush the autumnal blooms, scanning the bay windows of the guest house as she went, hoping to catch a glimpse of Helen's glossy golden hair to justify her suspicions.

She was halfway across the front lawn when a car door slammed in the street behind them. She froze like a deer in headlights until Matt hooked his arm around her waist and dragged her behind a hedge of neatly clipped privet. Her breath came in jolts; the pounding of her heartbeat in her ears blotting out all other sound. However, her reaction had nothing to do with the fact that their presence could have been discovered and everything to do with the fact that Matt's lips were inches from hers and he was looking at her with his 'come-to-bed' eyes that sent ripples of desire through her veins.

She let out an involuntary giggle at the ludicrousness of the situation. *What on earth were they doing here?* Was she really about to kiss Matt whilst they were secreted in a hedge and undertaking an impromptu surveillance of a random B&B? She chanced another glance through the glossy leaves at Matt whose arm, she realized, was still around her waist, and she knew there was nothing she wanted more. So what if it was unconventional – hadn't Matt taught her that she should squeeze every ounce of enjoyment from every adventure, from every minute of life? Who liked predictable, anyway?

She could smell Matt's cologne lingering into the air between them, sending her emotions into a maelstrom of anticipation. She leaned forward and when her lips met his, a shudder of pleasure rushed through her chest and radiated out to her extremities. Her thoughts scooted back to the last time they had kissed, on the beach after a spontaneous splash in the sea, and her heart fluttered with affection when she remembered it had been a prelude to sharing their painful childhood memories, of losing their fathers and the fallout that devastating experience had caused. From that day, she had known that Matt was more than a friend, and someone she hoped would be in her life for a long time. Forever even – especially if he continued to kiss her in the same way as he was at that precise moment, even if it was surrounded by prickly foliage!

A sudden flutter of bird's wings sent a spasm of shock shrieking through Rosie's veins and she pulled away from Matt, a wry smile curling her lips.

'Come on. I think we should get out of here before anyone sees us!'

'Wait! Look!'

She followed the direction of Matt's eyes to the upstairs bay window. A glint of sunlight sparkled in its reflection and highlighted a flash of movement from inside. Before she had chance to ask Matt if he had seen it too, a splash of scarlet appeared at the window. Even with the foliage masking her view there was no doubt as to the identity of the figure. Rosie gasped, but her surprise was nothing compared to the shock she experienced a few seconds later when a man appeared, wrapped his arms around Helen's shoulders and pulled her close to his chest.

'Oh, my God!'

Confusion raced through Rosie's mind. Who was this person? Did Helen have friends or family in Willerby? But this was a B&B, not a private home. Then another thought occurred to her. If she *had* arranged for someone to shoot Rick – then were they looking at her accomplice? No, that didn't explain why Helen was embracing him in full view of the street.

'Matt, I think we should leave, now. I feel like a character in Midsomer Murders!'

'I agree. Come on.'

Rosie tossed a final glance up to the window and pushed herself out of the hedge, rubbing her palms over her arms to eradicate the ripple of goose bumps that were running riot across her skin. What if Helen saw them loitering in the bushes? What would she think?

As Rosie stepped out from her concealment, a quiver of crimson caught the corner of her eye and she heard voices.

'Quick!'

Now it was her turned to drag Matt into the hedge, receiving a painful scratch on her forearm for her trouble, and they watched as Helen and her friend emerged from the front door – hand in hand! The couple walked down the front path, within a metre of their hiding place, then disappeared through the gate into the street.

Matt swivelled round to peek over the leaves and Rosie did likewise, her heart thudding out a melody of excitement – after all, this was her first 'stakeout'! mingled with the dread of being discovered. She wasn't sure if it was exhilaration or nausea that was causing her breathing to become so shallow.

The couple paused at the Porsche, the man reaching forward in a gallant gesture to open the driver's door. Helen smiled affectionately at him before jumping inside, revving the powerful engine and disappearing from view. Her companion remained on the pavement, running his fingers through his thick, silver hair as though pondering his next move. He stroked at the stubble on his jaw, clearly oblivious to the scrutiny of his audience. Eventually he turned and continued down the street in the opposite direction to the guest house until he reached a sleek white Audi TT.

Not the ideal vehicle of choice of your freelance hitman,

mused Rosie, raising herself up onto her tiptoes so as not to miss a thing.

The man yanked open the door and was about to climb inside when he paused, swinging his head towards the B&B, as though sensing their observation at last. Rosie ducked her head and took a hasty step back into the garden, the heel of her boot squashing a cluster of impressive polyanthus fireglow. Perspiration bubbled at her temples and her heart flayed at her ribcage with panic.

'Did he see me?' she hissed in Matt's ear.

Was he already marching back down the street to investigate, ready to thrust an arrow into her back as she ran for her life? Or would he tackle Matt first? Wrestle him to the ground before plunging a knife into his chest? Thankfully, Matt severed her stream of thought before she could conjure up any more gruesome scenarios.

'No, I don't think so, but I think we should get back to the café. I don't know about you, but I want to be there when Helen hears about what happened to Rick so I can watch her reaction.'

Rosie heard the Audi's ignition catch and the engine roar away. Within seconds, she and Matt were tearing back to the car park at the Drunken Duck and racing towards the Windmill Café, all thoughts of their romantic encounter on the back burner. As they navigated the narrow country roads at speed, Rosie tried to sculpt a plausible, innocent theory from the events she had just witnessed, but as the café grew nearer each hypothesis became more unlikely than the last.

Still, there was one thing she knew for certain. Even if Helen hadn't arranged for Rick to be incapacitated, she definitely had secrets to tell, and the sooner they spoke to her about them the better.

Chapter 8

Rosie jumped out of her Mini Cooper just as Helen was walking towards the terrace of the café and she broke into a run to catch her up. However, she was too late to stall her because Phil appeared at the door, his face a picture of shock, then panic.

'Oh, erm, Helen, I...'

'Phil? Brad? What's everyone doing here? I thought you were hiking to Garside Priory after the camp?' asked Helen, her eyes bouncing around the sombre gathering in the café. She reached up to twist her long, honey-blonde hair into a top-knot and secure it with a sparkly clip she had taken from her pocket. She radiated cheerfulness – her cheeks displaying a healthy glow and her lips perfectly outlined into a scarlet Cupid's bow – and it looked like no one was in a hurry to spoil her mood.

Clearly her meeting with the silver-haired stranger has raised her spirits, thought Rosie. What a shame her bubble of contentment was about to be burst big-style by her next question.

'Where's Rick?'

'I'll put the kettle on, shall I?' suggested Mia, heading towards the kitchen.

'I'll help you,' added Steph.

Rosie cast a glance in Phil's direction and saw him shake his head, a clear indication that he expected her or one of the others to inform Helen of her husband's unscheduled visit to the hospital. She looked over to where Emma and Brad were slumped together on the sofa, both studiously avoiding catching her eye. She sighed – the poor woman had been kept in the dark long enough, so she grasped Helen's elbow and guided her towards one of the Windmill Café's overstuffed white leather sofas and sat down facing her, sympathy suffusing through her body for the shock she was about to deliver.

'Helen, I'm sorry, we've been trying to contact you all morning but your phone must be switched off.'

'Oh, yes, silly me. I often forget to turn it on first thing in the morning. What ... what did you want me for?' At last, it had started to sink in that all was not right and Helen flicked her eyes nervously around the group as her anxiety began to mount. 'What's happened?'

'It's Rick. He's had an accident.'

'Oh my God! What kind of an accident? Is he okay?'

'He's fine, he's fine. It's probably just a flesh wound, nothing serious.'

Matt, who had followed her to the café in his SUV but had paused in the car park to take a phone call, appeared at the French doors and Rosie heaved a sigh of relief. For the briefest moment, his bright blue eyes lingered on hers before he strode towards Helen, his palm outstretched, with Freddie bringing up the rear.

'Helen Forster? I'm Matt Wilson. I own Ultimate Adventures and I led the hike to the Garside Priory this morning. I'm so sorry about what has happened. I've just spoken to the hospital. They've X-rayed Rick's ankle and diagnosed a displaced fracture which means he'll need surgery. He has to wait for the swelling to go down before they can operate so he could be in there for a couple of days.'

'But ... I don't understand. What happened? I've just got back from the village to be told he's had an accident ... what ... what kind of an accident?'

Before Matt could answer, Brad jumped in, the corners of his lips pulled into his cheeks as he struggled to keep the smirk from his face. If Rosie hadn't known better she would have thought he was enjoying his friend's misfortune.

'He was shot with an arrow. Our esteemed chairman does nothing by halves!'

'An arrow?'

Helen's hand flew to her mouth, her fingers trembling on her lower lip. Her eyes widened and her face drained of all colour beneath her expertly applied mask of expensive cosmetics. She stared at Matt in confusion, and then turned to Rosie, her lower jaw working overtime as she struggled to understand what Brad had said and formulate her next enquiry.

'Someone fired an arrow at Rick? You mean like a bow and arrow?'

'Yes.'

Helen flicked an incredulous glance at Phil, then Emma, clearly expecting them to tell her it was all a joke, a switch-around of the pranks Rick regularly played on them, and Brad, and no doubt all the other members of the Myth Seekers Society.

'It's true,' said Emma, an involuntary shiver rippling through her body as she took the seat on the other side of Helen. 'I'm so sorry, Helen. We found him this morning collapsed in the middle of the cloister at Garside Priory with an arrow sticking out of his leg. It was ... well, it was horrible.'

'Oh my God!' cried Helen, her jaw loose, disbelief scrawled over her soft features. At last the tears began to course down her cheeks leaving pale tracks in her foundation. 'I've ... I've got to get to the hospital.'

'Of course. A taxi is waiting in the car park to take you over to Norwich immediately. I'm sorry, there's no point trying to ring Rick,' added Matt, seeing Helen extricate her phone from her handbag. 'His phone's out of battery. Also, I should warn you that I've just taken a call from the police and they're on their way over there to talk to him.'

'The police want to talk to Rick?'

'Well, I suppose they'll want to talk to everyone.'

'What about?'

Rosie thought she detected a ripple of fear in Helen's voice, and if it were possible her complexion blanched even further – which only served to encourage Rosie's creative theories that Helen, or her friend, were in some way involved in her husband's accident. She conveniently ignored the fact that Helen appeared genuinely stunned at the news, putting it down to her being a very good actress.

'They'll need to establish exactly what happened, and to

ask us whether we saw anything unusual either this morning or last night that might give them a clue about who could be responsible.'

'If you'll excuse me, I just need to...'

Helen jettisoned from the sofa and rushed towards the Windmill Café's bathroom, her face so white she looked like she'd just endured an hour of root canal work, yet the clacking of her stiletto heels on the white-washed wooden flooring sounded incongruously jolly. As she reached the door, Steph met her carrying a large silver tray laden with a fresh cafetière of coffee, eight mugs and a plate of homemade shortbread balanced on the top.

'Oh, Helen, I'm so sorry about Rick. I thought you'd like a...'

Helen ignored her and ran into the Ladies'.

'I can't face eating or drinking anything until I know Rick's going to be okay!' declared Emma, getting up from the sofa and linking her arm through Brad's. 'I'm going back to the lodge for a lie down. Are you coming, Brad?'

'Sure.'

'I think I'd like to go back too, Steph,' mumbled Phil, his jawline rigid from the strain of trying to keep a lid on his emotions. 'To be honest, I'm absolutely exhausted with all the emotional turmoil. I could really do with a nap.'

Rosie suspected Phil wanted to leave so he could have a good cry in the privacy of his lodge, but she didn't blame him. In fact, she felt exactly the same – a bout of tears would definitely ease the tension that had been mounting since they'd discovered Rick.

With a sigh of relief, she waved off her guests, saw a pasty-faced Helen settled into the back seat of the taxi, and then returned to sit with Mia, Matt and Freddie at one of the tables in the empty café. She inhaled a long breath, relishing the faint fragrance of Flash, its familiar aroma soothing her nerves and settling the rampaging bewilderment that had threatened to send her to her own bed. She scanned her beloved café, appreciating the extreme order she always craved when life got too complicated.

'Well, I don't know about you, Matt, but I could definitely do with a mug of that coffee Steph and Mia made – and I've never been known to refuse a slice of your homemade lemon shortbread, Rosie,' announced Freddie, kneeling down at the table to pour them each a drink, his customary cheerfulness lifting the mood.

'Me neither,' said Matt, his smile of gratitude for his friend's offer cancelling out the smudges of tiredness beneath his eyes. Rosie saw the glint of mischief in Matt's eyes and knew that he was joking, but of course, the situation was far from a joke; it was deadly serious, as his next few words proved. 'I have it on good authority that shortbread can cure a multitude of ills, including the potential devastation of a person's business. I didn't want to announce it to everyone before, but when the police called earlier they told me that the centre has to close its doors until the person who shot Rick is caught. I'm so sorry about all this, Freddie, and to you too, Mia. I know how much you were looking forward to getting started on your training.'

'Don't worry, Matt, Ultimate Adventures will come through

this,' said Mia, biting into a piece of shortbread, catching the crumbs with her palm so as not to freak Rosie out. 'Just like the Windmill Café did. And do you know why?'

'Why?' asked Freddie, forgetting about Rosie's crumb-vigilante tendencies and sending cascades of sugar onto the table. Rosie fought her demons for a mere two seconds before declaring their victory and reaching for a cloth. She was just too tired to wage war on her foibles that day.

'Because Matt and Rosie are going to team up again and solve the Case of the Divergent Arrow, aren't you? I saw that gleam in your eye, Rosie, when you were watching Helen's reaction to Rick's accident. Am I wrong?'

'So you're reforming Willerby's crime-busting duo again?' asked Freddie.

Matt smiled at the enthusiasm in his best friend's voice. 'Mia's right, as usual. Rosie and I *have* talked about asking a few questions to see if we can solve the mystery before I totally drag my father's reputation through the mud, or we go bankrupt from lack of trade. But just because we've done it once, doesn't mean we'll be as successful in identifying the culprit this time.'

Silence descended on the café as they each considered the implications of what had happened to Rick during an Ultimate Adventures expedition and what the fallout would mean.

Rosie cupped her coffee mug in her palms and took an appreciative sip, watching Matt out of the corner of her eye as he ran his fingers through his blond spiky hair. Her heart contracted in sympathy for what he was going through, but the emotion she was experiencing was more than that. Matt was the one who had challenged her to stop wallowing in the mist of misery that her break-up with Harry had caused. He had taught her to simply stitch her heartbreak into the fabric of life and live alongside it, gathering new memories, collecting new experiences, making new friendships to embroider over the top. He had helped her to realize that happiness could co-exist with sadness.

And, she was happy to report she was getting there. Life was a journey not a destination and she was beginning to enjoy the ride again, especially when she had friends like Mia, and Freddie and Matt, to share it with. She was proud to say that her go-to reaction when she woke up in the morning was a smile, and that she could at last see her future as an arrow-straight road, rather than a tangled web of lingering resentment over the way Harry had jilted her for someone else. She knew it was time to let someone new into her heart, just as her sister Georgina had done with Jack – a soulmate with whom she could share her life and trust with her future.

'You know, Rosie, before you took over the Windmill Café, nothing interesting ever happened in Willerby. Matt and I even managed to sneak away on a few weekend fishing trips. Next thing we know, you parachute into our midst and we suddenly find ourselves right in the middle of another exciting episode of The Willerby Whodunnits.'

Rosie laughed. 'Nothing to do with me this time, Freddie, but I'm more than happy to step into the shoes of John Watson if Matt wants to go all Sherlock again and investigate what happened over at the Garside Priory. After all, I want to return the favour.'

'Me too,' added Mia.

'Me three!'

Freddie helped himself to a celebratory slice of shortbread, but this time he copied Mia by placing his hand at his chin and then tossing the crumbs into his mouth.

'Okay,' said Matt, turning his head away slightly as he took a gulp of his coffee to hide the swirling emotions his friends' loyalty had caused. 'Did either of you see anything or *anyone* suspicious on the trek over to the priory?'

'No.'

'No.'

'What I don't understand is how we all slept through your alarm, Matt,' mused Freddie. 'It's never happened before and we've done dozens of wild camping trips.'

'Actually, Matt and I have a theory about that. We think someone must have put something in our coffee.'

'Are you saying we were drugged?' cried Mia, coffee spluttering from her lips. She peered into the bottom of her mug as if expecting to see the remnants of a sedative. 'Are you serious?'

'It's the only explanation.'

'Oh, my God! You're absolutely right. Didn't I tell you that my brain felt a little bit fuzzy around the edges when I woke up, like it was filled with strawberry blancmange? I was fine once we'd started on our trek to the priory and the fresh air worked its magic, so I didn't think any more about it. Who do you think did that?'

'Well, it has to be that moron, Rick, doesn't it?' spluttered Freddie, his tone not only indignant but angry. 'He obviously wanted to be the only person in the group to witness the sunrise through the stone arch so that he could lord it over everyone at their Myth Seekers meetings and goad them about sleeping through it. We all saw how he went on during the camping trip, didn't we? How he spent the whole time belittling his fellow club members, vying to be the leader of the group in everything they did?'

'It does sound like the sort of thing he'd do,' added Mia, her eyes widened in disgust.

'It makes perfect sense,' continued Freddie, on a roll with his deductions. 'I think he set his own alarm, then, safe in the knowledge everyone else was out for the count, he set off to watch the sunrise and whoever is responsible for his murder was either waiting for him at the priory or followed him there.'

'It's possible,' said Rosie, knowing that if the two incidents were unconnected, Freddie's theory was the most viable. 'Rick is definitely more than just an enthusiast when it comes to myth-chasing. He's totally obsessed with everything to do with legends and folklore, and not just in the UK either.'

'So what fairy tale was Rick researching in Norfolk?'

Rosie paused for a second before leaping in. She knew Freddie held no truck with fables, legends and myths, preferring straightforward no-nonsense facts. He wouldn't be interested in stories about the ghost of a Brown Lady or the spirit of a disgruntled monk wandering around the priory waiting to shoot an unsuspecting visitor in the foot. But then she glanced at Matt, his eyebrows raised high into his forehead, his face suffused with interest. Unlike Harry who had made it his mission to sneer and deride every suggestion Rosie made to improve their Pimlico flower shop's business, she knew that Matt would listen carefully to her thoughts, however off-the-wall, and give them careful consideration.

'Well, there's...'

'No, no, let me have a guess! Maybe one of Robin Hood's ancestors galloped over the fields, shot Rick with an arrow because he'd invaded the priory's sacred ground, and then hared off back to Sherwood Forest? Or perhaps it was the tree fairies from the Isle of Man who followed him over here, bided their time as guests of the elves in the surrounding woods before wreaking their revenge for the time he trampled on their flower beds or gate-crashed their toadstool tea party? Oh, what if it was a ghostly black feline who attacks anyone who dares to trek across the farmer's fields?'

'I think Brad said it was a dog...'

'What dog?'

Rosie realized a little too late that she would only be digging her hole deeper by continuing.

'Never mind...'

'However,' interrupted Matt, rolling his eyes at Freddie before his expression became more serious. Rosie knew Matt wouldn't make fun of her and her confidence edged up a notch. 'If the two incidents are connected, and I think they probably are, then Rick can be struck from our list and the spiking of our coffee is something altogether much more ominous.'

'What do you mean?' asked Mia.

'Well, another scenario to consider is that the assailant put the sedative in everyone's bedtime drink apart from Rick's, and, knowing he was the type of person to take advantage of the situation and maybe get up earlier than everyone else to hike up alone, followed him at a distance and shot him when he entered the grounds. They then hid the bow and returned to camp where they woke up with everyone else to find Rick gone. Perfect alibi – for everyone.'

Rosie glanced at Matt and a spasm of heat spread from her chest to her face. His deep blue eyes, framed in long curled lashes the colour of straw, held hers for what seemed like an eternity. It took immense effort to drag her thoughts back to the present.

'When you spoke to the police, did they mention whether they'd found the weapon yet? The bow?'

'DS Kirkham said they were sending a team to search the area but as you know, the woodland is dense over there. I don't suppose anyone mentioned an Olympic gold medal in archery when they checked in, did they?'

'No.'

'So, if we rule out the four of us, we have five suspects,' said Rosie, keen to start whittling down their list before the closure of Ultimate Adventures could have a detrimental impact on Matt's business. She briefly wondered whether she should have said six suspects, to include the man they had seen Helen with that morning, but the conversation had rushed on.

'Five? There were only four members of the Myth Seekers Society with us, including Rick. I make that three,' said Freddie, his forehead creasing into parallel lines.

'What about Helen? And Steph?'

'Oh, it couldn't have been Steph!' declared Mia. 'She's lovely. Why would she want to hurt Rick? I'm sorry but I just can't see her holding a bow and arrow and shooting anyone – even someone as obnoxious as Rick Forster.'

Rosie had to smile as she pictured Steph in her Laura Ashley dress, her feet planted firmly apart as she drew back the string of a recurve bow and aimed an arrow at Rick's puffed out chest, like the Crazy Housewife of Nottingham.

'All sorts of people are driven to malice, Mia.'

'And Helen, I don't think...'

'We shouldn't rule anyone out,' interrupted Matt. 'Rosie, can I ask you a huge favour?'

'Of course.'

'Would you be able to arrange some sort of cookery classes in the Windmill Café tomorrow, like you did last time when we were trying to gather information about Suki's poisoning, something that everyone can join in with?'

'What? Why?'

'Well, it's better than everyone sitting around drinking tea and speculating on who shot Rick, isn't it? It'll keep their hands busy and their minds on something else – and people are much more forthcoming with gossip when they're involved in cooking.'

'No problem, Mr Holmes!'

'And is there any chance of rustling up something decent to eat now, Rosie?' asked Freddie. 'I'm starving!'

Chapter 9

Rosie's stomach growled in objection to her lack of consideration for either breakfast or lunch. She checked her grandmother's silver watch and was shocked to see that it was six thirty. No wonder Freddie was hungry! She and Mia set about making a huge pan of Bolognese sauce and the delicious aroma of baking bread and childhood nostalgia – it was her father's favourite meal – tickled her nostrils. She watched Mia stoop forward to slide a magnificent garlicky focaccia, pricked with sprigs of fresh rosemary and dripping with warm olive oil, from the oven, a smile playing at her lips when she saw her friend's apron.

'Loving the seashells theme, Mia.'

'Oh, no, they're not seashells, they're snails!'

Mia lifted the hem of her apron to show Rosie who tried her utmost not to grimace. Who in their right mind would want to wear an apron covered in snails, even if they weren't real? Well, only Mia Williams of course.

'Looks like you've cooked for the five thousand. Why don't we extend our hospitality to the guys over at the lodges? Helen will still be at the hospital so that's just an extra four?'

'I'd say that's a very generous gesture, Matt, if I didn't know you have an ulterior motive,' said Rosie, her wooden spoon poised above a steaming pan of spaghetti. 'But I agree, it's a great idea to sit down together to eat. I'm sure everyone is exhausted from all the emotional turmoil and can't be bothered to cook.'

'Great! I'll hop over and fetch them!'

Mia cast aside her tea towel and dashed from the café on her mission of culinary mercy, her ponytail swaying like a pendulum behind her. Rosie was relieved to see that the morning's escapades hadn't had a lasting effect on her friend's mood, and that her face had recovered its natural bloom whilst they had been engaged in their favourite activity. Mia gave the impression to everyone who was fortunate enough to cross her path that she was older twenty-three. From spending the last year travelling around Asia and blogging about it, she had developed a maturity beyond her years. After the initial shock of discovering Rick's crumpled body at the priory, she had simply rebooted her modem and joined in with the task of ensuring everyone was fed and watered and Rosie was proud of her.

Rosie picked up the discarded tea towel and hung it on its designated hook, aware that Matt was following her every move whilst he busied himself setting the table next to the French doors with the Windmill Café's peppermint-and-white china and silver cutlery. However, before he could say anything about her addiction to tidiness, their guests had arrived.

'Rosie, Mia, this is fantastic, thank you,' said Steph, who

looked amazing in a magenta, scarlet and cream belted dress and a purple angora cardigan with pearl buttons.

'Freddie and Matt helped too,' smiled Mia. 'And we've made two huge apple and cinnamon pies for dessert and a jug of homemade custard. Or you can try a slice of the sticky toffee gingerbread with lemon icing that Rosie and I baked yesterday.'

Rosie set out eight china bowls on the island unit and filled each one with a mound of spaghetti before Mia topped it with a dollop of rich Bolognese sauce, a sprinkling of freshly grated parmesan and a few fresh basil leaves. Everyone carried their food to the table and dug in with relish.

'Delicious!' declared Brad, as a flick of tomato sauce landed on his cheek and Emma reached over to wipe it away with her thumb.

A swirl of contented chatter rotated around the café's circular walls, just as it had every day of the week until recently, and soon every last morsel was hoovered up. Rosie wondered if it was right to be enjoying a fragrant meal whilst one of the lodge's guests was lying in the hospital waiting for an operation on his ankle, and another was having to endure the distress of seeing her husband in agony, but they had to eat to keep going.

'So, when do you think the police will want to question us?' asked Brad, a note of apprehension in his voice. 'I think they'll want to know all about our Myth Seekers Society, don't you? Phil, maybe we should take a look at the minutes of our last few meetings just to refresh our memories. I take it you've brought your laptop with you? And I reckon they'll also need to see the accounts. Why don't you print everything off so it's ready just to hand over when they ask? Perhaps there'll be something in there that can point the police in the direction of who did this to Rick.'

Phil looked up from his plate of spaghetti. Unlike everyone else, he had barely spoken a word during their meal, twisting the strands of spaghetti round and round with his fork whilst Steph looked on, her face a picture of spousal concern.

'What's up, Phil?' asked Emma. 'You look like you lost a pound and found a penny?'

'Excuse me,' Phil gulped, his face pasty white and tinged with an unattractive hue of green around the gills as he shot towards the bathroom.

'Poor Phil. He's never been interviewed by the police before,' explained Steph, helping Rosie to clear away the plates and hand out the dessert bowls.

'None of us have,' countered Emma. 'It's a scary prospect.'

'There's nothing to worry about,' said Freddie, as though he was a seasoned expert. 'Just tell the truth and everything will be okay. We all want to find out who did this to Rick, and the sooner we do, the sooner the cosh can be lifted from Ultimate Adventures. Now, I don't know about you but there's nothing better to calm the soul than a generous slice of Rosie's famous apple and cinnamon pie with lashings of custard.'

Despite their anxiety, everyone, including Phil when he returned, polished off two portions of pie each and then retired from the table to the comfort of the overstuffed white sofas. Rosie finished wiping down the worktops and storing every utensil and pan in its correct place before pouring herself a coffee, adding a drizzle of cream, and going to stand at the French doors.

Darkness pressed against the glass, turning it into a blackened mirror which reflected the activity within, giving the impression that the café was filled with twice as many guests. She took in the immaculate grounds, lit with a necklace of solar lights winding like stars along the pathways to the car park and the holiday lodges. A shiver ran down her spine as she imagined a dark spectre of malevolence stalking the fields beyond those doors – until that shiver turned into fear when she realized that the 'spectre' might be sat amongst them.

She closed her eyes briefly in an effort to crush down the rising panic, trying instead to conjure up happier memories of the times she and Mia had spent in the kitchen whipping up cupcakes, whisking meringues, slicing pineapples and mangoes. She inhaled a deep, steadying breath and eventually her heartrate returned to normal as the sweet aroma of warm sugar and caramelized apples sent a welcome blast of pleasure into her brain.

'Have you always wanted to be a chef, Rosie?' asked Emma from behind her, clearly keen to steer the conversation away from the approaching police interrogations.

'I've loved baking ever since I stood on a wooden stool at my grandmother's side helping her to beat the butter and sugar for one of her signature Victoria sponge cakes. But, actually, my childhood dream was to qualify as a solicitor like my dad.'

'So why didn't you?'

'I lost my dad when I was fourteen, so I decided to pursue

my second passion instead. We lived above a bakery so I had plenty of free tutorials in the holidays!'

Rosie laughed, but the sound rang hollow in her ears. However, she had no intention of explaining to Emma that after her father had passed away, her mother had been so consumed with grief that she had let the household finances slide to the extent that their house was repossessed. With the help of her father's brother, her Uncle Martyn, they had paid off all their debts from the proceeds of the sale and bought a tiny flat in a different part of Hampshire which had meant moving schools. Leaving her friends and the teachers who understood why her studies had slipped had been one of the most difficult things Rosie had had to deal with and she knew it was at the root of her continuing issues with cleanliness.

'Actually, I'm glad things worked out this way. The thought of being hemmed into a glass cube of an office, hunched over a desk overlooking the rooftops instead of trees and green fields holds little appeal. I love it here in the little Windmill Café, I love the friends I've made in Willerby, and I love our nights out at the local pub, the Drunken Duck. Even though being a café manager wasn't on my list of career options at school, it's a dream come true!'

'I totally agree with you,' said Emma. 'We should be allowed to change our career paths if we want to. I was brought up by my aunt and she's never been happy with my choices. She hates that I work at a gym. She hates my friends. She even hates my current choice of hair colour. She says I should appreciate my "gorgeous copper waves", but who's happy to be tormented for being ginger?'

Clearly Emma had overlooked the fact that she had the same colouring as Rosie did.

'She absolutely freaked out when I dyed my hair, but why shouldn't I be allowed to express my individuality? She criticizes the way I dress, the jewellery I wear, even my choice of perfume. And don't get me started about her views on my taste in music! We can't be expected to live out our family's dreams for us – it'll only destroy who we really are.'

Rosie saw a flash of something she couldn't fathom shoot across Emma's face and she wondered what had happened to her parents. However, she wasn't going to find that out tonight because Emma had grabbed Brad's arm and dragged him towards the door.

'Thanks for the dinner, Rosie. I think we'll leave you to your coffee.'

'Yes, I think we should go back to our lodge too,' said Steph, hooking her arm through Phil's and leading him gently in Emma and Brad's wake. 'In the circumstances, I don't think we could have asked for a better evening. Thank you, Rosie.'

'You're welcome. Hopefully we'll have some more information from the police in the morning.'

'Hopefully,' said Steph, not altogether convinced that was a good thing.

'I really don't think I'm going to get much sleep tonight,' muttered Phil, strands of his mousy hair fluttering in the breeze as he stepped out onto the veranda. 'My brain's jangling so much it'll take me ages to drop off. Got any of those herbal sleeping tablets you swear by, darling?'

Rosie closed the door behind them and turned towards Matt, Freddie and Mia.

'Did you…'

'We heard!'

'So we definitely can't strike Steph or Phil from the list! And they could have done it together – Phil could have doctored the coffee, whilst Steph could have done the shooting.'

'It's certainly another theory.'

Unsurprisingly, despite the lateness of the hour, Rosie didn't feel ready to say goodnight to her friends and climb the spiral staircase to her flat above the café. Matt must have seen her anxiety and as usual came to her rescue.

'Rosie, why don't you and Mia go upstairs and freshen up? I think a trip to the Drunken Duck will do us all good, don't you, Fred?'

'You know me, never say no to a pint at the Duck!'

'Thanks, Matt.'

Rosie almost wept when she saw the expression of gratitude on Mia's face as she skipped from the room. If she were a betting person she would wager that Mia would be back downstairs, ready to leave in five minutes.

She was wrong – it was three.

Chapter 10

Rosie struggled to decipher her emotions as she drove to Willerby in her battered Mini Cooper. Freddie had offered Mia a lift, which she had been thrilled to accept, and Matt was driving in his own Ultimate Adventures SUV so she had a few moments to herself to collect her thoughts and yet she could make no sense of them. It had been a long and emotionally draining day, and she couldn't wait to hold a glass of red wine in her hands to soften the peaks of her anxiety.

The Drunken Duck was straight out of central casting as the response to a Hollywood director's demand for a typical English village pub. Its white-washed façade shone in the moonlight and the bold golden signage glowed under the soft light of the brass lanterns. Only a few vehicles dotted the adjacent car park, so Rosie hoped she would find some privacy in which to unburden her constantly circling questions and increasingly outlandish theories about what had happened at the Garside Priory.

She loved what the landlord, Archie Chapman, had achieved with the Drunken Duck. Matt had told her that Archie had used the compensation money he'd received after his medical discharge from the army to buy the Willerby village pub. Prior to his arrival, the place had become frayed at the edges, catering only to a smattering of locals and day-trippers wanting sustenance before their assault on the coastal pathways or after a strenuous day of team-building at Ultimate Adventures. In the space of just twelve months, Archie had turned the fragile old lady into a sparkling duchess with regular offerings of guest beers from local artisan breweries, and even a selection of sparkling wines produced in the UK.

Rosie parked her car next to a pristine white Range Rover and jogged round to the front door. On the scrubbed stone step was a silver bowl filled with fresh water for the hiker's best friend and when she stepped over the threshold, she was immediately draped in the familiar mantle of warmth, comfort and the unquestioning welcome she experienced every time she visited. The fragrance of burning logs, pine cones and yeasty beer hung in the air and sent her senses into overdrive.

'Hi Archie. Can I get a glass of Merlot, please?'

'Coming right up.'

'And a pint of Wherry for me,' said Mia, sliding onto the bar stool next to her.

'The drinks are on me tonight, girls. Mia, is it true that *you* found the guy who was shot over at Garside Priory?'

'Yes, that was me. You know, the image of his body just lying there, with an arrow sticking out of his foot and blood oozing through his trousers, will remain with me until I take my last breath. I actually thought he was dead!'

Mia inhaled a long draught of beer that would have made a seasoned member of the Campaign For Real Ale proud.

Rosie was initially taken by surprise, until she remembered that Mia had been a student and then a gap year rambler for the last five years, and could probably drink her under the table.

'Come on, let's grab a seat in the snug,' said Rosie before Mia could spill every detail to the inquisitive landlord.

They carried their drinks into the back room and Rosie heaved a sigh that they had the place to themselves. However, no sooner had they sat down than they had company.

'Hi, Rosie! Hi, Mia! I didn't expect to see you both in here tonight,' smiled Grace, Reverend Coulson's daughter. 'Mind if I join you? I just needed to escape the frenzied activity in the vicarage kitchen for a christening Dad's doing at the church tomorrow. I don't mind helping out, but Mum's insisting on directing operations as if it's a military manoeuvre instead of a christening for triplets.'

The hug Rosie received from Grace was filled with such warmth, she was surprised to find that tears had gathered along her lower lashes. Grace would probably think she was being ridiculous but she couldn't help it, her emotions were all over the place – understandable after the day she'd had, she argued in her defence.

'So, I hear you're in the middle of another murder mystery!' said Grace, her grey eyes sparkling with interest as she plopped down onto the leather banquette next to Rosie, sipping her pint of Wherry, and shoving her blonde curls behind her ears.

'No one was murdered, Grace...' began Rosie.

'Oh, why didn't I insist on tagging along with you both on your wild camping trip instead of volunteering to make up the flower arrangements in the church? I always miss out on all the excitement. So, you've got to tell me everything! Josh told me that Matt and Freddie arranged the expedition to Garside Priory for a group of ghost-hunting enthusiasts who are staying at the lodges. He and Archie are already arguing over who could have shot Richard Forster, but you were both there – eye witnesses! Who's on *your* list of suspects?'

Grace replaced her pint on the bashed copper table and swung her eyes eagerly from Rosie to Mia and back again, rubbing her palms down her jean-clad thighs and causing her diamond solitaire to glint in the overhead lights.

'It's too early to make any assumptions...' said Rosie but she was instantly interrupted by an excited Mia who was acting as though they were in some kind of am-dram theatre production in which the whole village had been assigned roles.

'Well, my money's on Phil Brown – he has the strongest motive for wanting Rick out of the way. All the guests at the lodges are members of some nerdy Myth Seekers club in Manchester. Phil used to be the club's chairman and lead ghost whisperer until Rick arrived on the scene and elbowed him from the top spot. Apparently, Rick took over every aspect of the running of the club, apart from the accounts which he was happy to leave to Phil because, let's face it, they're *boring*.'

'Wow, looks like you've really thought it through!' said Grace, who had been slowly shredding a beer mat whilst digesting everything Mia had said. She collected the fragments of paper in her palm and aimed a throw at the log fire, but her aim fell short and the tiny pieces of cardboard tumbled like confetti onto the hearth.

Rosie rolled her eyes and was about to kneel down to sweep the debris away when Matt arrived in the doorway of the snug clutching a pint of Guinness. She chastised her traitorous heart for leaping to attention at the sight of him. He had replaced his black Ultimate Adventures T-shirt and combat jeans with a lilac cashmere sweater and a leather jacket that moulded his muscular torso to perfection. Attractiveness oozed from his pores – or maybe that was just the effect he had on her as no one else seemed to have lost their train of thought when he'd appeared – yet the arcs of tiredness beneath his eyes spoke of the stress he was under.

'Any news?' Rosie asked.

'Helen rang me just as I was pulling into the car park. She's back from the hospital. They're hoping to operate on Rick's ankle in the morning, but she also said that Rick's thinking of giving an interview to the local press about what happened, supposedly to raise the profile of the myths and legends of East Anglia, but I'm concerned about the possible backlash.'

Matt slumped down next to Rosie, taking a long draught of his beer to calm his worries about the business. He ran his fingers nervously through his hair, his lips tightening into a smile that didn't reach his eyes.

'We have to find out who did this as soon as possible! I can't have the press sniffing around, dragging Ultimate Adventures into the spotlight, spouting rubbish about the health and safety risks of being shot by a stray archery arrow. You know how these journalists love to twist everything to get a sensational story out of the mundane. Imagine what they could do with this! You can bet your last pound they will say it was one of Ultimate Adventures' activities gone wrong, especially as we *do* happen to offer field archery courses and tuition – but we never, ever shoot after dark, or first thing in the morning!'

'Well, once you and Rosie put on your sleuthing shoes I'm sure you'll have the mystery solved before those reporters have had a chance to sharpen their pencils,' smiled Grace, raising her glass in a toast of confidence.

'Did Helen have any news on whether the police have located the bow?' asked Rosie.

'She didn't mention anything, and I didn't ask.'

'Could it have been one of the bows from Ultimate Adventures?' asked Mia.

'No, definitely not. I've checked our storeroom and everything is as we left it, thank God. It's not only my business I'm concerned about, though. This area of Norfolk needs all the visitors it can get. We don't want holidaymakers cancelling their trips for fear of an encounter with a rogue archer wandering round the woodlands picking off unsuspecting walkers and hikers at random.'

'So you think this was a random attack, do you?' asked Grace.

'No, I don't. I think Rick was the intended target. What I don't know is whether they just wanted to incapacitate him or if it was something much worse, but whatever the reason, its origins lie in Manchester and not Willerby or Ultimate Adventures.'

'Do you think it was one of the guys you took on the expedition to Garside Priory?' said Grace as Freddie joined them from where he'd been chatting to Archie and Josh at the bar.

'If you ask me, they all seemed a bit odd – Rick, Phil, even Brad and Emma,' said Freddie, taking a seat next to Grace. 'For a young couple in their twenties they were surprisingly fanatical about extending their spectrum of extreme sports. I'm not criticizing them – extreme sports are my life's work and I love every aspect of the outward-bound business and activities, but those two are seasoned adrenalin junkies, the more danger and the higher the risk, the better. Fell running, wild swimming, free climbing, and their addiction to running marathons borders on the psychotic.'

'Those hobbies don't come cheap, either,' added Matt, narrowing his eyes as he thought through what Freddie had just said. 'Insurance for a start is beyond most people's means. I'm not sure what they do for a living, but it has to be something that not only produces the funds but also gives them the flexibility to pursue their crazy goals.'

'So you have three suspects to get your teeth into?' asked Grace.

'No, five. I don't think we should rule out Helen or Steph.'

'Really? You think his *wife* shot him?'

'Well, wives do tend to be the ones with the best motives,' grinned Freddie, draining his pint and leaving the snug to fetch another one.

'Even if Helen's got nothing to do with it, we still need to talk to her to get some insight into what Rick's like as a person, although I can make a few assumptions about that without her help,' mused Matt. 'To be honest, when I spoke to her just now she didn't seem as upset about what had happened as I expected her to be, but that could be delayed shock. She told me she intended to take a sleeping pill and go straight to bed.'

Rosie flicked her gaze from the depths of her wine glass to Matt. Helen was the second person now to have referred to having sleeping tablets in their possession. But how could she have administered the sedative? And another idea occurred to her too. What if her silver-haired friend wasn't a hired hitman, but her lover? She wanted to run that new hypothesis passed Matt, but decided to adjourn her conjecture until the next day when she didn't have such an extensive audience and changed the subject.

'How are the wedding arrangements going, Grace?'

'If you'll excuse me, I think I'll get a refill before Archie calls last orders,' announced Matt with a grimace, almost sprinting away to the bar where Freddie was chatting to Archie and Grace's fiancé.

'With Mum on the job everything is progressing at lightning speed,' smiled Grace, shooting a look of complete devotion at Josh. 'Dad, of course, is overjoyed at being able to perform a wedding ceremony for his own daughter and he's been tweaking his sermon for weeks. I told him to keep it short – you know what he's like! And the village hall is going to look so pretty, even if it snows.'

'Well, getting married on Christmas Eve, you've got to plan for that possibility,' said Mia, her eyes sparkling with the romance of it all. 'Anyway, it'll all look amazing with a sprinkle of snow and garlands of fairy lights.'

'Mum's been baking since August. Our wedding cake is made, just needs to be iced. The cars are arranged, too. One of Josh's friends owns a vintage car hire company and insisted we have the pick of the crop. And, of course, Mum's friends from the WI have the floral side of things neatly sewn up. Josh's brother, Mark, is walking me down the aisle – well, Dad can hardly do it, can he? And his sister, Josie, and my friend who I went travelling with, Abbi, are my bridesmaids. Josh's parents are flying over from Hong Kong the week before, so that's it! Everything is organized.'

Grace scooted to the edge of her seat and met Rosie's eyes.

'You will come, won't you, Rosie? And you must bring a plus one, erm, if there is a plus one?' She raised her perfectly groomed eyebrows, a twinkle of mischief playing in her eyes. 'If you haven't got anyone you'd like to bring, then I'm sure Matt would be delighted to step in and be your escort for the day. He told Josh he didn't have a plus one sorted yet. I know how hard it will be for him to come to a wedding at St Andrew's church after what happened with Victoria, so it would be great if everyone rallied round to keep his mind off things – and I can see how well the two of you have been getting on.'

'I'm sure Rosie would love to attend your wedding on the arm of the extraordinarily handsome Matt Wilson!' beamed Mia, giving Rosie a blatantly lascivious wink.

Rosie rolled her eyes at her friend's transparent matchmaking efforts, but she was happy about being invited to Willerby's wedding of the year. Grace radiated happiness as she spoke of her approaching nuptials and she deserved her special day to go smoothly. Even though her father had a direct line to the orchestrator of their fates, the privilege hadn't protected the family from experiencing tragedy when Grace's younger sister Harriet had died from meningitis at the age of seven. It was a cruel grenade to toss into the lives of such wonderful people but Grace and her parents, Carole and Roger Coulson, had dealt with the agony with such dignity that they'd taught Rosie a great deal about coping with grief in all its guises.

'Thank you, Grace, it's very kind of you to invite me. I'd love to come to your wedding, and if you need any help with the food, or the flowers, you only have to ask.'

'Thanks, Rosie. So? Will you accept Matt's offer to escort you?'

'Erm, pardon?' spluttered Matt, arriving back in the snug to hear Grace's loaded question. His bright blue eyes filled with alarm, and Rosie realized immediately that he had intended to make an excuse not to attend the wedding at St. Andrew's church.

'Grace, is it really necessary to be escorted to a wedding in the twenty-first century? I mean, I can…'

'Great, that's settled then. I'll add you both to the guestlist, no need to RSVP. Okay. I'd better get back home. Mum wants me to help her bake another batch of scones for the Baby and Toddler group tomorrow. Bye.'

The light in the room seemed to dim in Grace's absence,

but the only thing Rosie noticed was the uncomfortable sensation of a steamroller reversing over her bones, and from the look on Matt's face she could tell that made two of them.

Chapter 11

Blades of autumnal morning sunshine sliced through the clear blue sky tantalizing those below with the promise of a crisp, dry day. Rosie stood at her bedroom window in the little windmill, listening to the rustle of the leaves in the gentle breeze and feasting her eyes on her favourite scene – one which she would never grow tired of appreciating.

London had its urban beauty and architectural magnificence, but the view from her flat above the Windmill Café won first place in the natural beauty contest. In the distance, the surface of the North Sea always echoed the weather of the day – some days dark and foreboding, angry even; others blissful and calm – but that morning it seemed to dance with a cascade of iridescent pearls. If she turned her head to the right she could see the luxury lodges nestled in the field next door like sleeping puppies wrapped in an emerald blanket and snuggled against the russet-coloured woodland in whose depths Ultimate Adventures was hidden.

A surge of belonging enveloped her, swiftly followed by one of gratitude for being accepted as part of the community of Willerby so quickly. She'd even been invited to her first wedding! With some difficulty, she tore her eyes away from the view, patted her childhood teddy bear for luck, and jumped into the shower. She selected her smart black dress trousers and a jade green sweater which enhanced her amber curls and slotted her toes into a pair of ballet pumps. With minimal attention to her make-up routine she took a final glance out of the window and trotted down the stairs into the café kitchen to whip up a batch of lemon drizzle cupcakes.

Baking was her solace; the antidote for when things became too much for her to cope with. Whenever she could focus her attention on beating a bowl of butter and sugar with a wooden spoon, she was able to block out all unpleasant and unwelcome thoughts and simply enjoy being in the moment – like a kind of culinary meditation. And it had the added bonus of not only bringing happiness to her, but to everyone who shared in the results of her labour.

She set the lemon cupcakes to cool on a wire rack, the aroma of caramel and tangy lemon causing her stomach to growl with anticipation. She had just finished washing the floor and was busy fixing a cafetière of coffee, when Matt appeared at the French doors.

'Mmm, that coffee smells amazing. Any chance of a mug?'

'Of course. Actually, I'm glad you came over, Matt. I wanted to talk to you about Grace's invitation yesterday. I know how difficult it will be for you to attend a wedding at St Andrew's after what happened with Victoria, so if you'd rather...'

'You're right, it *will* be tough to return to the very place I had the dubious honour of being a jilted groom, but with a little help from my friends I'm happy to report that I've moved on. In fact, being a guest at Grace and Josh's wedding is the perfect way of laying old ghosts to rest, once and for all. And there's no one I'd rather stand next to in those pews than you, Rosie.'

Matt took a step towards her, his eyes holding hers, his lips parted slightly. A whoosh of heat flew through her body, sending pins and needles out to her extremities and all cogent thought from her mind. Her knees weakened as he drew closer and she felt his minty breath on her cheek as he continued, his voice gentle and sincere.

'I know Freddie thinks you've brought a whirlwind of chaos to our lives since you arrived in Willerby, but without you I wouldn't have even contemplated stepping foot in the church. I know you came here for a fresh start, but your arrival has provided that to others too. I have a great deal to be thankful to you for, Rosie, not least your willingness to help me to find out who's trying to destroy my business.'

Matt's lips were millimetres from hers and her internal choir was screaming 'kiss me!' She inhaled a long breath, excitement and exhilaration curling through every part of her, her heart pounding in anticipation. Arrows of desire shot southwards and all she wanted to do was block out reality and melt into his arms.

'Matt, I...'

'Hello? Anyone home? Oh, hello, Matt! I didn't ... sorry, Rosie, I don't want to intrude.'

'It's okay, Phil, come on in.'

Rosie laughed as Phil's cheeks coloured when he realized what he'd stumbled in on. Could she really see him resorting to mastering the sport of archery simply to shoot the over-bearing and obnoxious chairman of his beloved club? Brad clearly thought so, but she was prepared to reserve her judgement until she had spoken to him, and what better time than the present. From the look on Matt's face she knew he was thinking exactly the same thing.

'Do you want to join us for a coffee? And I've made a fresh batch of lemon drizzle cupcakes, too. Actually, I was wondering if anyone in your group would like to come over to the café this morning for a tutorial in all things cake-related. It might help to keep everyone's minds off ... well, off everything?'

'I think the girls would love that, and so would I. I have to admit to feeling somewhat apprehensive about the impending visit from the police, but I'm just as anxious as everyone else is to find out who did this to Rick – mainly so I can shake the guy's hand.'

'I take it from that comment that you didn't like Rick Forster much?' asked Matt, handing a cup of black coffee to Phil before replenishing his own.

'No one liked him. He was rude, disrespectful, arrogant, opinionated, selfish; take your pick. He totally ruined our club!'

Matt indicated the table next to the French doors. 'I don't know whether you've heard, but the police have asked me to close the doors at Ultimate Adventures. It's not only my livelihood at stake, but that of Freddie and Mia, too, not to mention the trade my clients bring to Willerby – it's imperative that the mystery is cleared up swiftly. So, do you mind if Rosie and I ask you a few questions?'

'I don't mind at all. We all want to know the truth about what happened, but Rick was way out of line when he accused one of us of shooting him. Of course, I'm sure we all wanted to, but no one would have had the courage to do it!'

'Can you tell us a bit about the Myth Seekers club?'

'Before Rick arrived in our midst a few of us would meet up every month to talk about current topics in the myth-seeking world. We had the occasional aficionado come to speak to us from one of the other clubs – there's only a couple in the north of England – and it was all very civilized and relaxed. We didn't have a formal written constitution or elections for posts on the committee and such like. I dealt with whatever paperwork there was. I collected the subs and paid the rent for the hire of the hall to the parish council. It worked. We were trundling along nicely, minding our own business, not upsetting anyone. I'm a founder member and Brad joined a couple of years later and was appointed our official trip organizer, but we didn't have the funds to go very far. Not until Rick joined and flashed his cash – then we went to all sorts of wonderful places; Rome, Athens, Marrakesh.'

'Are there many myths to seek in Marrakesh?' asked Rosie, happy to see Phil's eyes light up at her question.

'Yes! It's a fascinating place. You wouldn't believe the things we...'

'So, along came Richard Forster to spoil the fun, is that it?' interrupted Matt, keen to divert Phil from a long-winded soliloquy on the marvels of North African folklore.

'Well, not at first. Rick's an accountant with a large practice in Manchester city centre. He's loaded so he offered to donate an injection of cash to boost our admittedly meagre funds. As well as chairperson and secretary, I was also the Myth Seekers Society's treasurer. Not a great appointment to be honest as I'm rubbish with figures.'

Phil paused to shove his tortoise-shell glasses up the bridge of his nose and shoot a quick glance in Rosie's direction, before he resumed his nervous habit of scrapping the skin from the sides of his thumb nails.

'Rick's money meant we could do more: take more trips, invite professional speakers, even print up a few flyers to encourage new members. That's how Emma heard about us and got together with Brad. Turned out they're both adrenalin junkies – speed cycling, snowboarding, marathon running – so they had lots in common. But after a while Rick started to take over. He appointed himself as our chairman and he insisted that every meeting had to start with a carefully crafted agenda. He typed up the minutes and we even had to vote on written resolutions. Okay, it meant we got lots more done but the whole atmosphere changed; it was more formal, less enjoyable.'

A wistful expression rippled across Phil's freckled face as he remembered happier times.

'And it wasn't just me who objected to the changes, ask the others. Most of the old-timers drifted away and there's only me and Brad and three others left from the pre-Rick days. But we've attracted ten new members who seem to accept the way things are. However, it isn't *our* club anymore, if you know what I mean. We missed the times when our get-togethers were really just an excuse for a chat, a break from our domestic obligations, and maybe a sneaky pint afterwards.'

Phil's hand trembled as he patted down his neatly cropped mousy hair. Watching his gesture, Rosie got the distinct impression he was struggling not to shed a tear for the loss of his beloved club which had been hijacked by the new boy. But after a few steadying breaths Phil was ready to continue.

'I'm afraid I was Rick's first target in his crusade of humiliation. I've been researching a book on obscure Welsh myths for years and he scoffed at my "jerky" writing style, telling me that no one would be interested enough to publish it. I've already self-published one book – okay, it's not brilliant, but that's no reason for Rick to humiliate me in front of the other members, is it?'

'So why didn't you leave too? Why stay and subject yourself to regular sessions of verbal abuse?'

'Because I happen to love the club. It's my baby. I suppose I thought some of the things Rick introduced were improvements, especially the foreign trips which I know he subsidized. I also know Rick paid for this weekend out of his own pocket, Rosie. There's no way we could have afforded a posh holiday site like this from our funds. It was his idea to come here and to combine our myth-seeking activities with the luxury accommodation for the women. Helen and Steph both love home-baking and afternoon teas in quaint little cafés – it's that Great British Bake Off fiasco. Rick said it would keep them out of our way so we could enjoy the trip without feeling guilty. Pff, guilty? I don't think Rick Forster has an empathic bone in his body.'

Rosie felt a squirm of sympathy for Phil. He seemed to be one of the good guys, and after all, she had witnessed first-hand the way Rick had laid into him at the camp. He would have her support if he wanted to dish out some of his tormenter's own medicine. Maybe he *had* intended to kill Rick for muscling in on his beloved club, but, like his writing style, his aim was 'jerky'.

'It's no secret Rick taunted me about a lot of things. Steph and I don't have the level of funds Rick and Helen are blessed with. But we've managed to raise three fine young men and we've been happy. Rick has been married twice before and, as far as I know, has never had children. I suppose he sees me as plodding and dull; an anorak, I think he calls me. Steph says he's a cowardly bully who is insecure in his own skin. She's forever telling me to stand up to him, to tell him where to go, but I have to think of the club's interests, don't I? If Rick left there'd be no more trips to exotic locations so I made the decision to just grin and bear it.'

Rosie tried to offer Phil a supportive smile but he was more interested in picking invisible fluff from the knee of his combat trousers. 'Phil, can I ask you how you felt when you woke up yesterday morning?'

'What do you mean?'

'Well, it's just that both Mia and I felt a little fuzzy-headed, as if our brains had been stuffed with cotton wool.'

'Actually, yes, yes, I did feel a bit woozy, like my feet were encased in concrete, but I've never camped out under the stars before. I prefer a sheet of canvas between me and the elements. I just put it down to a bad night's sleep.'

'I don't suppose you saw anyone leave the camp after you turned in for the night?'

'No. I was flat out until you woke us all up, Matt. I was ... well, I was annoyed that we had missed seeing the sunrise through the arch. It was the only reason I agreed to do the wild camping thing in the first place. I was furious when I found out Rick had gone ahead and had somehow engineered the whole debacle. But then I shouldn't really have been surprised, should I? It was the sort of thing he *would* do. It's all about him. It's always all about him.'

'And where were you when you heard Mia scream?'

'I was with Emma and Brad. They'd asked me to take a photo of them with the priory in the background. I was lining up the shot when I heard the commotion. We all rushed into the cloister and there was Rick, lying on the ground with an arrow imbedded in his ankle.'

'I know you would have mentioned it if you had, but did you notice anything unusual or suspicious during our trek to the site?'

'Nothing, I'm afraid. I've scoured my brain for every bit of information, but there's nothing. Look, Matt, Rosie, I make no secret of the fact that I loathe the man, but I didn't wish him any harm and I certainly don't know how to use a bow and arrow. Poor Helen, she must be really upset. Steph asked her if she wanted to share our lodge last night so she didn't have to sleep alone, but she turned us down. She's a braver person than I am, that's for sure. What if that crazy archer is still out there, training his arrow on us right at this very moment?'

Phil leaned forward, wringing his hands as he made a supreme effort to corral his emotions. Rosie watched on, her heart twisting for this man who had been repeatedly bullied by Rick Forster and who therefore had to be one of their chief suspects.

'Okay, I think Steph will be out of the shower by now. I'll inform her, and Helen and Emma, of your generous offer of a morning in the kitchen, Rosie, and we'll be across in half an hour or so.'

'Great, and look on the bright side, Phil. Rick's going to be out of action for a couple of months whilst his ankle heals, so maybe you should recommend he appoints a new interim chair?'

'Yes, yes, I never thought of that. I suppose I should.'

And as Phil pulled the French door shut behind him Rosie could have sworn she saw the tug of a smile at his lips.

'It's him!' she exclaimed.

Matt rolling his eyes at her and grinned. 'How did you deduce that, Miss Marple?'

'He has the strongest motive. We both saw with our own eyes the way Rick treats him – it was embarrassing to watch. Phil put up with it for so long; he was ousted from his beloved club, taunted with insults about his lack of funds, called nasty names, humiliated in front of the other members about his book, powerless to retaliate. Well, *I'd* shoot Rick if it was me! You can only push a person so far before they snap.'

'Mmm, possibly. So, say he does have a motive, what about opportunity?'

'Well, that's easy. Phil knew what Rick planned to do, so he spiked our coffee with a few of Steph's tablets to make sure we slept through everything, followed Rick up to the priory, missed with the first arrow, scored a hit with the second, then hid the weapon and jogged back to the camp to pretend to wake up with the rest of us.'

'I agree with you that Phil Brown is the sort of person who could spend many hours pondering over the finer details of how he would go about murdering Rick if he had the courage. But plotting it and carrying it out are two completely different scenarios. There's no evidence at all to suggest it was him.'

'He's definitely hiding something though.'

'What? And why?'

'It's just the way he couldn't meet my eyes when we were taking about how he felt about being pushed out as chairman and being given the poisoned chalice as treasurer. I'd have thought Rick was the ideal candidate for that post, being an accountant. So why did he let Phil keep that job?'

'Okay, I'll give Phil a call and ask whether he minds letting us have a look at the accounts and the minutes of the committee meetings Rick made them do. At least Rick's meddling in the admin of the Myth Seekers Society has produced *something* useful.'

'Why don't you try to call Rick again? He's had plenty of time to mull over the events at the priory whilst being confined to a hospital bed. Maybe he's remembered some vital detail, or reconsidered his initial reaction that it was Phil who shot him and can shed some light on someone else being the culprit. The more information we have about the actual shooting the better, don't you think?'

'Great idea – if he'll take my call. I've tried three times

already today. He's clearly holding me responsible, even though it wasn't me who actually held the bow!'

Matt removed his phone from his back pocket and selected Rick's number. He waited, his eyes lingering on Rosie's, but there was no reply and his call went to voicemail. He cut the call without leaving a message.

'I didn't think...' Before Matt had finished his sentence, his phone buzzed. He glanced at the screen and then at Rosie. 'It's a text from Rick.'

'What does it say?'

She waited whilst he read it, taking in the way his jawline tightened and his eyes narrowed before he shook his head disconsolately and handed her the phone.

'"*Matt, I've spoken to my solicitor who has advised me not to speak to you until the police have completed their enquiries in case our conversation jeopardizes any subsequent legal action. Rick.*" Oh, Matt. I'm so sorry.'

'Well, at least I know why he's been avoiding me. Now, if you'll excuse me, Rosie, I think I should go back to the centre to get on with some paperwork of my own.'

As Rosie watched Matt make his way from the café, her heart cracked at the dejected way he carried his body. A surge of irritation spread through her veins at Rick's decision to involve his lawyers so promptly, swiftly followed by an over-whelmingly intense desire to put on her metaphorical deerstalker and hunt down every last clue until the mystery was solved and things could go back to normal. A world in which Matt Wilson wasn't brimming with his habitual enthu-siasm and cheerfulness wasn't a world she wanted to live in.

Chapter 12

'Hi Rosie, what do we have planned for the Windmill Café bake-off this morning?' asked Mia, hanging up her crimson duffle coat and unfolding her apron – that day's was embroidered with what Rosie thought were gentlemen's moustaches but in fact turned out to be bats; at least the design was in keeping with the season.

'I thought we'd make a few batches of date and walnut scones and peppermint and dark chocolate chip cookies. What do you think?'

Rosie met Mia's eyes, and the smile disappeared from her face as she saw beads of tears sparkling along her friend's lower lashes. 'Mia, what's wrong?'

'Oh, nothing really.'

'Mia, something's happened. I can tell from your expression.'

'It's Mum. When I told her last night that it was me who found Rick she ordered me to stay at home today. She's convinced there's a serial killer stalking the area with a quiver full of arrows searching for his next victim. Nothing I could say would make her change her mind, but I admit I might have made it worse by telling her we're almost certain it's one of the people we've got staying in the lodges. She says the Windmill Café is turning into an adventure playground for crazy people and she doesn't want me to help with the Autumn Leaves Hallowe'en party on Saturday.'

'If you want to go home then it's okay by me, you know that, don't you?'

'No way! Rosie, I don't want to go home. I want to stay here with you and bake, bake, bake! But it means we've got to redouble our efforts to find out who did this or everyone might react like Mum and decide not to come to our party – and we can't let that happen, not after all the work we've put in!'

'Actually, I did wonder whether we should cancel the party.'

'No! Rosie, you can't do that! Please, let's just give it another couple of days. We solved the poisoning mystery, didn't we? We can do this too!' Mia pleaded.

'It's Tuesday. Do you think we can do that by Friday? I'm not sure we can...'

'Hi Mia. Hi Rosie. Oh, what a wonderful smell. Any chance of a quick coffee before we start baking up a storm?' asked Brad, stamping his feet on the mat before entering the café kitchen. 'I didn't get much sleep last night and I feel like a runaway juggernaut hit me straight on. Emma, darling, you really need to see someone about your snoring!'

'Pot and kettle, Brad, pot and kettle,' giggled Emma, standing on her tiptoes to deposit a kiss on his lips. 'Mmm, are these lemon drizzle cupcakes?'

Rosie took a few moments to scrutinize the young woman. Today's outfit would not have looked out of place on an

Olympic athlete; black Lycra leggings, vibrant green running vest, and a pair of very expensive trainers. Her hair had been styled with a smidgeon of gel, and she looked fresh and raring to go and her youthful vitality made Rosie feel exhausted. She gulped down a mouthful of her rich, dark coffee, closing her eyelids for a few second to savour the taste and to allow the aroma to spiral into her nostrils and the caffeine to do its work.

'Hello, everyone. Steph said we were having a baking lesson this morning?'

'Oh, hi Helen, yes, we are. How's Rick?'

'Complaining vociferously, but there's nothing unusual there. Unfortunately, his operation has been postponed until tomorrow so you can imagine what he said about that. He was so rude to me on the phone this morning that I told I'm not going to visit him today and you know what he said? He said, good, he could do with some peace and quiet. So here I am, ready and willing to experiment with anything that has sugar and buttercream in it.'

'Well, we're glad you're here. We're just waiting for Phil and Steph to get here, but why don't you put one of our Windmill Café aprons on and grab yourself a coffee?'

'Thanks.'

Rosie couldn't prevent her mind from scrolling back to the previous morning. The cookery class was the perfect opportunity to have a chat with Helen to see if she could persuade her to volunteer any information about who she had been meeting. Mia was right if they didn't sort this mess out quickly, people would choose not to come to their Autumn Leaves party – even though the incident had happened miles away from the Windmill Café – and that would be a tragedy.

By the time Phil and Steph had arrived and put on their peppermint aprons with the little white windmill logos, the sun had climbed over the treeline in the east and had gilded the terrace outside the French doors with a welcome glow. The curlews and the larks were well into their morning melody but the calm of the grounds belied the turmoil within Rosie's heart. Maybe Mia's mother was right and there *was* a murderer watching them from the woods.

Just as she always did in times of trouble, Rosie submerged herself in the rhythm of baking, of rubbing cubes of butter into flour, of adding milk a dribble at a time, of moulding the mixture into thick scones and baking them in the oven. The scent of warm sugar floated through the café and settled her emotions, so she embarked on an extra lesson on how to make the best shortcrust pastry for pies that they went on to fill with a compote of blackberry and apple and stewed pumpkin and cinnamon.

Everyone was laughing and having fun, and surprisingly Phil turned out to be a maestro at making pastry, beaming when everyone declared his efforts to be melt-in-the-mouth delicious, unlike Emma's soggy-bottomed attempts. Spirits were high as they turned their attention to the peppermint cookies, and Rosie found herself sharing a countertop with Helen, remembering her intention to engage her in innocent chatter. She briefly wished that Matt was at her side to guide her, but she grabbed her confidence by the scruff of the neck and launched in.

'So, have you and Rick been married long?'

'Two years – actually I'm Rick's third wife and I'm beginning to empathize with the other two.'

Rosie saw a tightening of Helen's jawline when she gritted her teeth and narrowed her eyes, no doubt recalling her phone conversation with Rick that morning. The man really did seem to have a talent for rubbing people up the wrong way. Helen paused in her task of rolling a ball of cookie dough, flicked her long mane of hair over her shoulder, and fixed her heavily mascaraed eyes on Rosie.

'Maybe it was one of his exes who shot him – I wouldn't blame them. Rick probably drove them to the edge of their sanity after years of boring them rigid with his never-ending garbage about mystical beasts, ghost-hunting and ley-lines.'

'I take it you don't share his interest in the Myth Seekers Society?' laughed Rosie.

'Are you kidding me? A bunch of middle-aged men sitting around talking about fairy stories? No, I don't share Rick's crazy obsession. You know, I'm surprised he hasn't got around to introducing compulsory costumes yet – wizard cloaks, pointed hats, magical staffs with special powers, or even insisting everyone grows matching Gandalf beards, although it's possible that Phil may have started on his attempt.'

Rosie cast a swift glance in Phil's direction and giggled. Helen joined in and it was quite a few seconds before they calmed down, after which she knew their mutual merriment had formed a friendship and she felt emboldened to ask the next question as she rolled out her shortcrust pastry.

'Do you and Rick have children?'

For a moment, from the expression on Helen's face, Rosie thought she had gone too far, that Helen was going to snap that it was none of her damn business and storm out of the café. However, as she continued to watch, Helen's shoulders slumped and a veil of sadness floated across her attractive face. When she finally spoke, her voice was strained, as though it was being forced through a sieve.

'Sadly not. I want children but Rick refuses to even discuss the subject. Nothing I say or do seems to change his mind. If he'd told me that *before* we got married I might have reconsidered our engagement. I don't know, but one thing I do know is that I want a child in my life more than anything. I'm thirty-nine now and my time's running out.'

'Does Rick have children from his previous relationships?'

'He has a child from his first marriage, but he split up with his wife a few months after the birth. He's never had any contact. I'm not even sure whether it was a girl or a boy. It's really sad. I've tried to persuade him to reconsider, but of course he refuses. His excuse is that he's too busy. He's a senior partner at Featherstone & Garner in Manchester, one of the city's largest accountant practices, and when he's not at work he's chasing spectres around the world.'

'I'm sorry, Helen. It must be a difficult time for you at the moment.'

Silence descended whilst they finished their bakes and slid them into the oven. The café filled with mouth-watering aromas and a swirl of animated conversation about more light-hearted subjects until the products of their labour were cooling on the wire racks, ready for the best part – the tasting.

'Helen? Phil, Brad and Emma are going over to the pub in Willerby for a drink. Do you want to go with them?' asked Steph, appearing at their counter, wiping her hands on a tea towels and removing her apron.

'Sounds exactly what I need, thanks Steph.'

'I'm staying here. I've got a bit of a migraine coming on from all the worry.'

'Oh, I'll stay with you if you want me to,' offered Helen.

'No, you go and have a drink. It'll do you good and I'll be fine.'

'Okay, see you later.'

'Bye, darling,' said Phil, kissing his wife on the cheek.

Rosie watched them leave with Mia bringing up the rear carrying a huge Tupperware box destined for the vicarage. She turned back to Steph and saw her face was flushed a deep shade of crimson as she dabbed a scrap of handkerchief at her eyes.

'Steph, what's the matter? Are you okay?'

'Not really.'

'Come over here and sit down. I know how distressing all this has been. Why don't I make us a pot of tea and we can have one of those lovely scones?'

'Thanks, Rosie'

Rosie busied herself with the kettle and the tea pot, racking her brain for an indication as to why Steph was so upset, but she couldn't come up with anything. She carried the tray to the coffee table next to one of the café's plump white leather sofas and handed Steph a mug of sweetened tea, the ubiquitous balm of choice for the distressed the world over.

'Is everything okay?'

'I've got to tell someone or I think I'll go crazy. I'm not sure what it means, if anything, but ... well, I saw Helen sneak out of her lodge late on Sunday night. There, I've said it.' Steph leaned back on the sofa and let out a long sigh of relief. 'I went to bed at eleven, as usual, but I couldn't sleep because Phil was away at the Ultimate Adventures camp so I got up to make myself a hot chocolate and took it out onto the veranda to look at the stars. That was when I saw Helen take the Porsche and drive towards Willerby, not first thing in the morning as she wants everyone to believe.'

'Really? Do you have any idea why?'

'Well, the first thing I thought was that she was missing Rick just as much as I was missing Phil and that she'd gone to join him at the ridiculous wild camping expedition. God, I couldn't think of anything worse! Rick told us all that we were here for a week of sightseeing and relaxation and the lodges looked so lovely on the internet that I agreed to tag along with Phil, but as usual, Rick had a totally different agenda. I knew there'd be some myth to track down, or some dark, dank dell to explore.'

'Well, as you know, Mia and I were at the camp and Helen didn't arrive.'

'I know.'

'So, where do you think she went?' asked Rosie, her brain cracking up as she tried to join the dots.

'I ... you're going to think I'm awful, but it's been whirling around my head ever since I heard about Rick's accident.'

'What has?'

'Helen could have driven to Garside Priory, shot Rick in the leg, then driven back to the village without anyone ever knowing she'd left her lodge.'

'Erm, well, yes, I suppose she could, but she didn't come back to her lodge, did she? She wasn't here when we all arrived back yesterday morning. Of course, everyone thought she'd gone out early in the morning, not the night before. And what makes you think she would do something like that anyway?'

'Well, there are a couple of reasons, one of which you know already. I'm sorry, but I overheard your discussion with Helen earlier. I know about her desperation to have a child and Rick's abject refusal to entertain the idea. Cruel, if you ask me. He should have made his views on the subject clear before they got married, don't you think? Or it could be the same old chestnut – Rick's very wealthy, you know.'

'You think Helen tried to kill her husband for his money?'

'A tempting proposition, and one I have to admit I've considered on many occasions, but I would never have the courage to follow it through!' announced Helen, who had appeared at the French doors and overheard the last sentence.

'Oh my God! I'm so sorry, Helen. What must you think? I...'

'It's okay, Steph.'

Helen came into the café and sat down opposite Rosie who could feel her face glowing with mortification. She took a long draught of her tea and let it dribble slowly down her throat to allow time for her heart rate to return to something approaching normal.

'Helen, I'm so sorry...'

'You're only saying out loud what other people are thinking, Steph. But let me tell you something. If I *had* decided to shoot Rick with a bow and arrow, I wouldn't have missed, but more importantly, I actually have a rock-solid alibi.'

'You do?' whispered Steph, at last able to meet Helen's eyes.

Rosie knew exactly who Helen's alibi was, and the pieces were starting to fall into place. She hoped Helen was about to confess the details of her rendezvous with the handsome silver-haired stranger so she and Matt could at least strike one person from their list of suspects.

'I do, but if I tell you, can it remain confidential between us, please?'

'Well, I'm not sure...' began Rosie.

'Oh, and of course, I'll be completely honest with the police when they get around to questioning me. It's just – I hope that won't be until after Rick's operation. He's a bastard but I don't want him to find out before he goes under anaesthetic. I would never forgive myself if anything happened to him.'

'Okay, our lips are sealed,' said Steph, fully recovered and sitting on the edge of her seat like an eager puppy waiting for a treat.

'I was with a friend in a B&B in Willerby.'

'A friend?'

'A male friend.'

'Oh.'

'His name's Tim Latimer and he's a partner at Featherstone & Garner.'

'A colleague of your husband's?'

'Yes.' Helen lowered her lashes briefly to study her perfect manicure before meeting Rosie and Steph's gaze head-on, a look of defiance burning in her eyes.

'You're having an affair?'

'Yes.'

'Oh.'

'We've been seeing each other for six months. Tim's the complete opposite to Rick. He's actually interested in me as a person; he buys me flowers and chocolates, takes me to art galleries and the theatre when Rick's off on one of his jaunts. I feel like a real woman when I'm with him. Tim and I want to be together and I'm going to ask Rick for a divorce.'

Helen couldn't hang on to her emotions any longer and they spilled over in a deluge of tears. She leaned forward and covered her face with her hands as Rosie rushed into the kitchen to fetch a box of tissues and an extra cup.

'Thank you.' Helen accepted a tissue and a mug of strong, sugared tea. 'I don't love Rick anymore, but I didn't shoot him. I've spoken to Tim and he's quite happy for me to give the police his details so they can confirm I was with him from midnight on Sunday night until ten-thirty on Monday morning – if you found Rick at eight o'clock on Monday morning then we both have alibis.'

Rosie contemplated Helen for a few seconds before grasping her hands and giving them a squeeze. Helen had a difficult few weeks ahead of her but Rosie found herself hoping that her new friend would find happiness with the gentleman waiting for her at the B&B in Willerby. And maybe the child she so patently longed for.

Chapter 13

Rosie allowed herself a smile when she pulled into the car park at Ultimate Adventures, the memory of their 'almost' kiss still fresh in her mind. The familiar crunch of the tyres on the gravel was music to her ears because it meant she was about to spend time with Matt and Freddie, two of her favourite people in Norfolk.

Of course, she hadn't always felt so upbeat about arriving at the outward-bound centre. In fact, for the first three months of being in Willerby, she had steadfastly avoided gracing the wood-built headquarters for extreme sports with her presence. The very thought of flinging herself from a flimsy platform suspended ten metres from the ground filled her with horror, not to mention the sight of the mud-caked quad bikes lined up outside the storeroom waiting for a rider to take one of them for a spin.

She had changed a great deal since arriving at the Windmill Café and she sent up a missive of gratitude to her guardian angel who had obviously just returned from a gap year. Six months ago, all she could think about was the heartbreak of witnessing her then boyfriend familiarizing himself with the intimate requirements of one of their bridal clients. Now, here she was, assisting a friend in uncovering the truth behind an incident that could affect the future of his business.

Rosie's thoughts then flicked to her father and how proud he would have been of her, not just for coming to a friend's aid in solving the mystery, but also for having the self-confidence to even think she could do such a thing. All she had left to work on was her predisposition to recoil at the sight of clutter; something she was about to face imminently when she entered Ultimate Adventures' office and kitchen.

'Hello? Anyone in?'

'Oh, hi Rosie, great to see you. Fancy a coffee?' asked Matt, indicating the kettle with a nod of his head.

'No, thanks, I've just had one at the café.'

She averted her eyes from the jumble of washing up crammed into the sink and concealed a shudder of anxiety. She fought an almost overwhelming urge to grab a cloth and start wiping down the crumb-scattered benches – until she saw the state of the cloth! Fifty shades of grey came to mind – she wondered whether the kitchen had ever seen a spray of bleach. However, she hadn't driven to Ultimate Adventures to spend the day cleaning.

'Are you here for that zip wire ride you've been promising to try?' asked Matt, a dangerous twinkle in his eyes. 'No better time than when we're closed to the paying public.'

'You know that's never going to happen, right?'

'Never say never! Okay, so what about a quad bike safari? I thought I'd take the opportunity whilst we're closed to give the bikes a good clean, but...'

'Matt, I've come to tell you that we can strike off two people from our list of suspects. I've been doing a bit of ... well, I suppose my father would have called it cross-examining, whilst we were baking this morning.' She inhaled a long breath and relayed the details of her conversation with Helen and Steph. 'So, we can definitely discount Helen and her friend Tim Latimer.'

'Good work, Ms Watson. And you'll be pleased to know that I haven't been slacking in the amateur detection arena either. As soon as I got back here, I called Phil and asked about taking a look at the Society's accounts. He was a bit hesitant at first, but relented when I told him that if we could identify Rick's assailant quickly, the police might not need to question everyone. After seeing the books, I can understand his lack of enthusiasm.'

'What do you mean?'

'It seems the Myth Seekers Society isn't what you would call flush with funds. In fact, the accounts are in a complete mess. Phil was right when he told us he wasn't the best book-keeper, but it's more than incompetence. Looks like our reluctant treasurer was helping himself to the money. Not a lot, and only two withdrawals, but still, if Rick found out about it I'm sure he would have wanted to expose him in the most humiliating way possible.'

'And Rick's an experienced accountant. It wouldn't have taken him long to discover any discrepancies,' added Rosie, not surprised to find she wasn't enjoying the turn of events. She didn't really want someone as nice as Phil to be the potential culprit.

'Exactly.'

'So, do you think Rick threatened to report Phil to the police for stealing from the members? That Phil decided to silence him and like everything else he does, he bungled it?'

'Well, it's a bit of a leap, but it's a possibility, don't you think?'

'Okay, let's talk to him about it, if only to rule him out as well.'

She pushed her chair back, anxious not only to ask Phil about what Matt had found out, but also to get out of the cluttered room where she felt as though the walls were starting to close in on her, debris flying from the surfaces and whipping her emotions into a maelstrom of panic. Her heartbeat had quickened and this time it had nothing to do with Matt's proximity and everything to do with the mess. However, before she was able to escape, Matt grabbed her arm, his face serious.

'Rosie, I want you to know how grateful I am for your support. I haven't told Freddie or Mia, but I've had to cancel five lucrative, corporate team-building expeditions this week and unless we open again by the beginning of next week, Ultimate Adventures will slip into the red. We need a minimum of three bookings every week to stay afloat. I've already fielded a couple of calls from Dan Forrester at the Willerby Gazette wanting an interview about what happened and asking whether we intend to offer any more wild camping trips this season. I wasn't going to tell him that we've actually got another two planned before the end of November, because once this fiasco finds its way into the press we can kiss goodbye to those bookings too. It's an absolute disaster.'

Rosie's stomach swooped down to her toes and back when she saw the anguish on Matt's face and she was even more determined to uncover the truth than she had been before. She grabbed her phone and before Matt could refuse, she dialled Phil's number.

'Hi, Phil, it's Rosie here. Thanks for sending the accounts over for Matt to take a look at. Would you mind if we asked you a few more questions? We could come over to your lodge or you could drive up to the office at the outward-bound centre – bring Steph if you want.'

'Okay. I won't pretend I wasn't expecting a call. We'll be with you in thirty minutes,' sighed Phil, making it clear that he would rather swim naked in the North Sea in the middle of winter.

'Great, see you then.' Rosie turned to Matt with a wide smile. 'Simple.'

'Thanks, Rosie. I owe you. I admit I had a bit of a dip in my usual effervescent self-confidence – it won't happen again. To show you how grateful I am, I'll rustle up the coffee because I totally understand your reluctance to enter the war zone that is the Ultimate Adventures kitchen.'

Rosie listened to Matt crashing and banging around in the tiny kitchen as he prepared their drinks. She cringed when she thought of having to pretend to enjoy his offering without actually taking a sip. Unless Matt and Freddie had had a complete personality transplant since the last time she was there, she didn't want to imagine what state the mugs would be in. She was about to start the counting exercises her sister Georgina had taught her for whenever she felt overwhelmed by her hygiene monsters, but just then she saw Phil's battered old Volvo drive past the window.

'They're here!'

Rosie went to greet Phil and Steph at the door of the wooden reception lodge and wasn't surprised to see that Phil's face had drained of whatever little colour he had. He hesitated on the threshold, nervously pushing his spectacles up to the bridge of his nose and fiddled with the numerous zipped pockets of his combat trousers. For once, he didn't have his camera slung around his neck and he was clearly at a loss to know what to do with his hands.

'Hi, thanks for coming over. Matt's in the kitchen making some coffee for us. Why don't you grab a seat and I'll tell him you're here?'

'Thanks, Rosie,' smiled Steph, ushering her husband towards the pine table in the corner of the room. She smoothed the skirt of her peach-and-mint printed dress over her buttocks and sat down gingerly on the flimsy plastic chair.

'Thanks for letting me take a look at the Myth Seekers Society's accounts, Phil,' began Matt as he placed the tray carrying the coffee mugs onto the heavily scarred table before going off to collect his laptop.

Phil looked like he was on the verge of tears. His lips parted to reply to Matt, but no words came out. Steph grabbed his trembling fingers and raised her chin so she could face Matt and Rosie head on. Rosie could see from the expression on Steph's face that she knew exactly what Matt had found in the books and had taken the decision to speak about it before being asked to justify the irregularities.

'Phil was given the unenviable task of being the Myth Seekers club treasurer, but he has never professed to be the world's greatest bookkeeper. Heaven knows why Rick didn't just take over the whole damn society, especially as accountancy is his area of professional expertise. Richard Forster isn't a very nice person, as I'm sure you have discovered already. He's a bully who dishes out disparaging remarks like confetti, not only to Phil, but to Brad and Emma and most of the other long-standing members – some of whom felt they had no option but to leave. But Phil and Brad love the club so they stick it out. Yes, the accounts are a mess and Phil would bring the books home and worry himself stupid about them.'

'And the two unauthorized withdrawals?' asked Matt, getting straight to the point.

'They were to pay for a plaque to commemorate the Myth Seekers Society's twentieth anniversary,' said Phil, casting a quick glance at Rosie. 'Brad and I followed the correct procedure for its proposal as laid down by Rick's recently introduced written constitution; we drafted a resolution, submitted it to the committee – which was quorate – and put it to a vote. It was rejected because Rick didn't want it to go ahead, probably because it wasn't his idea – and he held the casting vote.'

'So why the withdrawals?'

'I was determined to mark the anniversary. I know it was wrong, but I went behind Rick's back and ordered the plaque anyway. It was more expensive than I had anticipated and I couldn't afford it myself, so I paid for it out of the Society's funds. I admit I made two unauthorized withdrawals – the first was for the deposit and the second was to pay for the plaque on delivery. I broke the rules. Rick found out and threatened to report me to the police for theft.'

All the while he spoke, Phil studied his fingernails in his lap. Now that he had confessed his crime out aloud he glanced across at Steph, his eyes brimming with tears, but he seemed to gain strength from her unwavering support.

'I know what I did was wrong. Rick insisted it was his duty to inform everyone in the club what I'd done, and that he *had* to follow the written procedures laid down in our constitution for such misdemeanours which was to report the matter to the authorities. He only postponed his trip to the police station because he didn't want to spoil Helen's weekend treat. I know all this makes it look like I have a jolly good reason for wanting to get my own back on Rick, but I had nothing to do with what happened, I swear.'

'Of course you didn't, darling,' said Steph, her expression indignant. 'Look, Matt, my husband's a decent and honest man, who's never even held a bow and arrow, never mind used one. Rick Forster was an arrogant dictator who made plenty of enemies, in his professional life as well as his personal life. I have no doubt Rosie has filled you in on how he has treated Helen? That man takes an inordinate amount of pleasure from victimizing and belittling good people who perhaps aren't as accustomed to the cut and thrust of life in the fast lane as he is. I think we should be looking in a different direction for the person responsible for shooting him.'

Steph sat back in her chair and folded her arms, a challenge in her eyes – which melted like a chocolate fireguard when

Matt said, in his usual imitable way, 'I agree with you, Steph. Can you tell us about your own movements yesterday morning?'

'*My* movements?' Steph spluttered, her soft, powdery features stretching in surprise at the unexpected question. 'I didn't shoot Rick if that's what you are implying! I dislike him tremendously but I wouldn't sink so low as to make him part of my life in any way. These people are best ignored in the hope that they'll crawl back under the dark dank stone they came from!'

'So, your movements yesterday?'

Steph stared at Matt, then looked at Rosie with incredulity.

'Steph, dear, you've got nothing to hide. Tell him.'

'Well, as you know, Helen and I were the only guests still at the lodges on Sunday night. I couldn't sleep so I decided to make a cup of hot chocolate and that was when I saw Helen disappear in the Porsche. I went back to bed and my alarm woke me at seven-thirty as usual. I showered, dressed and made myself some breakfast then snuggled up on the sofa to read my book. That was when I noticed the note Helen had pushed through the door saying she had gone to the village which she clearly wanted me to discover first thing in the morning. We all know where she was, don't we?'

'So no one can vouch for your whereabouts between 10 p.m. and when the camping group returned to inform you that Rick had been shot?'

'Well, I ... well ... no, I suppose...'

'Let's just think this through for the sake of conjecture. You could have driven out to the priory, shot Rick as an act of revenge for the way he treated your husband and to stop him from reporting his discoveries to the police, then returned to your lodge without anyone knowing you had left.'

'Now wait just a minute, Matt! Steph's a committed pacifist, she even insists that I carry spiders outside instead of washing them down the plughole. Really, I must insist...'

'Sorry, Phil, but this is the sort of thing that the police will be considering when they interview you.'

'Really? And how is Steph supposed to have mastered the intricacies of bowmanship? It's not something you can do without intensive training, you know. And although the first arrow missed, the second was pretty accurate.'

'That's a very good point. I'll definitely make some enquiries about archery clubs in the Manchester area.'

'Good!'

Silence descended and the atmosphere was as thick as treacle. Unlike Matt, Rosie was a great believer in intuition and her gut instinct was telling her that neither Phil, nor Steph, had anything to do with Rick's shooting. Both of them had had ample opportunity to cause Rick harm in a much easier fashion than going to the trouble of learning the correct way to hold a bow. However, they couldn't discount Phil or Steph just yet. Then another idea pinged into Rosie's head.

'Can I make a suggestion, Phil?'

'What?'

'It looks like Rick's probably going to be in hospital for the next few days at least, and then he'll need some time at home to convalesce. I think if you were to re-present your resolution for the commemorative plaque to a newly-convened committee

– without Rick in attendance – the proposal might be carried in your favour, wouldn't you agree?'

'Yes, yes I do. Thanks, Rosie, I'll do that. Look, find out who did this, will you, so we can all get back to normal.'

'Don't worry, we're trying our best,' muttered Matt, downing the last dribble of his coffee and returning his mug to the tray with a clatter.

In a reversal of their arrival, it was Phil who lead Steph from the wooden cabin, his arm around her waist, whispering platitudes as he went. Matt, on the other hand, dropped his head into his hands and Rosie groaned in frustration too.

'So, that went well,' said Rosie.

'True, this mystery-solving lark is a lot harder than you think! We still have four suspects on our list with excellent motives for wanting Rick out of the way – none of whom have alibis – and we've still got Brad and Emma to talk to.'

'Hang on, I thought we'd discounted Helen and Tim?'

'As they've provided each other's alibi, don't you think there's a possibility they could have done this together?'

'Oh, yes, I never thought...'

Rosie's head began to throb. One step forward, two steps back! How proud would her father be now?

Chapter 14

'Fancy a drink at the Duck?' asked Rosie.

'Love one.'

'Why don't you leave your car here and I'll drive. Would you mind if I swing by the windmill to collect a jacket? I might walk home later.'

'No problem, although I'd be happier if you ordered a taxi.'

'In case I get shot by an arrow?' Rosie teased, meeting Matt's eyes and feeling her heart give a bounce of attraction.

She thought back to the afternoon they had spent by the sea at the end of August when Matt had chased her through the waves, splashing freezing water in her face, and how the day had ended in them kissing on the beach. That had been the day they had bared their souls to each other, pouring out their personal histories, discovering that behind any calm exterior, turmoil and heartache can reign supreme until you find the courage to banish the demons that occupy the darker corners of the mind.

Since that day, her relationship with Matt had steadily deepened and whenever she was in his company she knew they had achieved a mutual understanding of what had happened to make them who they were, but it was so much more than that. For the first time since she'd broken up with Harry, Rosie felt she could let someone into her heart and she craved the opportunity to repeat the kiss they had shared in the bushes outside the B&B in Willerby. Talk about unconventional! But that was what made their relationship all the more interesting.

'I'll wait in the car, just in case I have an allergic reaction to the intense smell of chlorine you've got going on in the café,' Matt joked, but she saw the gentleness in his eyes.

Like Mia, Matt was aware of her struggle with the cleanliness ogres. She had also confided in him that the catalyst had been the loss of her father and the ensuing wrench from the comfortable life she had known until then. But, with the help of her sister, and after meeting Harry and hoping that he would be her partner for life, the monsters had crawled back into their grim, angst-ridden boxes for a while – only to return six months ago when she had found Harry rolling around amongst the dahlias and the chrysanthemums with Heidi.

Fortunately, working in a café environment meant it was easy to deflect curious enquiries about her over-the-top obsession with hygiene as a respectful regard for the Health and Safety regulations, and she had managed to hide it from all but the most observant of onlookers. She knew she would have to relent to her sister's encouragement to seek counselling one day, but she wasn't ready to talk through her issues with a stranger just yet. However, with the constant friendship and support she had found in Willerby that possibility was starting to peek its head above the parapet and demand attention more regularly.

'Okay, I won't be long.'

Rosie jogged to the windmill, wondering whether she should get changed and try to do something with her unruly waves, but she discarded the thought immediately. Neither Matt, Freddie or Mia cared about what she looked like. They loved her for who she was, not whether her hair was twisted into a perfect chignon or her eyelashes were coated with lashings of dark brown mascara. However, she did decide to give her new cashmere cardigan an airing.

She opened her bedroom door and the shock rushed at her with a vengeance. Her hand flew to her chest and she gasped in horror. Without waiting, she spun on her heels, tumbled back down the spiral staircase and sprinted to the car park, her breath coming in ragged spurts both from the sudden onslaught of exertion and the fright.

'What's going on?' asked Matt, jumping out of the passenger seat before she arrived, his face creased in concern.

'I ... well, I think it's probably better if I show you.'

Together, they rushed back to her flat and, swallowing down her fear, Rosie pushed open her bedroom door. She pointed to the white rattan chair next to the window where her collection of soft toys was enjoying the view – apart from the careworn bear she had loved for twenty-eight years who now had an arrow protruding from his brown furry chest. The sight was so unnatural that she felt physically sick, but she knew her reaction would not have been so severe had any of her other bears suffered the same fate. Mitzy held a special place in her heart because he had been her father's childhood bear and, ridiculous though it sounded, she felt as though someone had entered her private inner sanctum and attacked a member of her family.

A spasm of dread rippled through her veins and sparkled out to her fingertips. She opened her mouth to say something to Matt but the words caught in her throat and she had to sink down onto her bed to catch her breath.

'I'm scared, Matt. Someone's obviously been in my flat, *in my bedroom*, while I was with you at the outward-bound centre. Do you think it's because we've been asking questions about what happened to Rick? Perhaps the person responsible thinks they're about to be discovered and this is their way of warning us off? Oh God, excuse me!'

Rosie dashed to the bathroom but managed to hang onto the contents of her stomach. She splashed her face with cold water and spent a few moments pulling herself together.

'Let's go downstairs and I'll make us some tea,' said Matt. 'Then I think we should report this incident to the police straight away. They'll probably want to come over and take a look tonight.'

In mute acquiescence, Rosie followed Matt down the stairs to the café. She watched him make his call to the police and then fill the kettle, warm the pot, and pour out two mugs of strong tea, feeling as though she was floating from the ceiling watching actors perform a stage play on the ground below. She smiled her thanks, but the sight of the thick brown beverage turned her stomach and she rushed outside to the terrace to inhale huge gulps of the cold, autumnal air until her ears pricked up at the sound of conversation.

'I'm bored, Brad! *You* might think it's fun being cooped up in a tiny kitchen baking a few twee cakes to pass the time, but I don't. Why can't we go home, or at least spend the day windsurfing or riding the zip wire over at Ultimate Adventures?'

'You know the centre is shut!'

'So what?'

Rosie watched Emma stalk towards her on the terrace. Displaying an expanse of naked chest under her lime-green Gore-Tex running hoodie, she looked like she was ready to launch straight into a marathon along the North Norfolk coast. There wasn't a spare inch of fat on her slender frame, testament to her addiction to extreme sports. Brad, who had remained where he was, unsure whether to follow his girl-friend, also rocked the muscular and toned look, and Rosie noticed again how heart-churningly attractive he was – they made a perfect couple.

'Oops, I'm sorry, Rosie, I didn't mean to...'

'It's okay, Emma. Actually, Matt's here at the café. Why don't you ask him if he's got any suggestions to keep boredom at bay? I'm sure there's lots of adrenalin-pumping activities to choose from if you're prepared to travel a bit further afield.'

'Awesome, that's more like it. Is there an indoor archery range, too? Steph told us you and Matt were planning to call a few as part of your on-going "investigations"?'

A smirk tweaked at the corners of Emma's mouth when she highlighted the word investigations with her fingers. Satisfied she had hit her mark, she dashed inside the café and plonked herself down on the sofa next to Matt, stretching out her legs, flexing her trainer-clad toes and lifting her sinewy arms above her head before running her fingers through her hair. Brad hesitated for a moment before deciding that it was a good idea to give Emma some space, shrugged at Rosie, and turned to go back to the lodge.

'You're so lucky, Matt. Brad and I would love to work somewhere like Ultimate Adventures, but we always try to join in with every extreme sports challenge we can – gorge scrambling, canyoning, free climbing, orienteering. We also did the Three Peaks challenge last month with a couple of friends who joined one of your team-building courses last year, so when Brad told me Rick had arranging a trip down here for the myth seekers to visit some ancient stones or other, well, I was straight on to it. I didn't think I'd be forced to sit through a cookery tutorial, though. No offence, Rosie.'

'Well, actually I *did* ask ... never mind.'

Rosie caught Matt's eye. He gave her an almost imperceptible shake of his head, clearly hoping that she would let Emma talk in case what she said shed some light on her involvement with the group. However, after what had just happened in the place she called home, she couldn't think straight. Questions were rotating through her brain like bingo balls in a tumble dryer.

How long would the police take to get there? Would they want her to vacate her flat? Would they expect her to go to the police station to give a statement? Had Emma and Brad been hanging around outside the café, waiting for her to return home and find her poor teddy bear speared by an arrow? Were they there just to watch her reaction? Or was the perpetrator concealed in the Willerby woodland with a pair of binoculars trained on her every move? Or an arrow?

Thankfully, before Rosie could pose any more improbable questions and drive herself closer to the precipice of her sanity, Emma continued with her exuberant chitchat.

'Matt, Brad and I didn't get chance to tell you how much we enjoyed the wild camping expedition. It was worth the sacrifice of spending a couple of hours mooning over a bunch of boring old stones just to be able to camp out in the open, staring up at the stars. It's awful what happened to Rick, especially after he subsidized the trip, but I hope it doesn't stop him from organizing other expeditions. Brad and I could never afford to stay anywhere as luxurious as this on our wages.'

'So is that the only reason you tagged along?' asked Matt.

'Well, do I look like the sort of person who enjoys searching for non-existent vibrations radiating from a bunch of rocks? Brad loves that side of things, but not me. I admit that I'm in it for the subsidized jaunts. This year alone we've been to the Isle of Man and Scotland, even to Athens and Marrakesh!'

'How long have you guys been together, then?' asked Rosie, anxious to perform the role of cross-examiner that Matt had assigned her despite the fear burgeoning in her abdomen.

'We've only been dating for about seven months so we're not living together yet. I share a flat with two friends in Manchester. Both guys – for some reason I seem to have more of a connection with men than I do with girls.' Emma smiled at Matt from beneath her eyelashes and Rosie couldn't stop herself from rolling her eyes. 'Brad still lives at home with his parents, would you believe?'

'Where do *your* parents live, Emma?'

'I never knew my father. He left Mum when I was a baby and she brought me up until she died when I was ten, and then I went to live with my aunt and cousins. Three boys. That's where I get my love of sports from; the more extreme the better! My cousins used to take me camping and climbing in Snowdonia. We spent weekends abseiling and free-climbing, and I've even flown down the longest zip wire ride in Europe. It'd be a dream come true to work for an outward-bound company.'

'Where do you work at the moment? Even subsidized trips abroad don't come cheap.'

'I work as a gym instructor. Pay's okay. Brad helps me out a bit sometimes.'

'Mia and I were just talking about Sunday night and whether we might have seen anything unusual. Did you or Brad notice anything untoward when you went to collect the water from the stream?'

'Well, I wasn't really taking much notice to be honest, but if there had been something, I think I would have pointed it out to Brad, so no, I didn't.'

'And what about the last time you saw Rick before we found him in the cloister?'

Emma flashed a look at Rosie. 'Same as everyone else, I guess. I remember you and Mia crawling into your tent...' Rosie saw the glint in Emma's eyes that said 'wimps', '...and the rest of us huddled down for a night under the stars in our sleeping bags – including Rick. The next time I saw him he was lying in agony in the middle of those ugly stones with an arrow poking through his foot. It could have been anyone of us, and when I think about it, I absolutely freak out. It's just too awful!'

'So you weren't disturbed at all during the night?'

'No.'

'And how did you feel when you woke up?'

'Yes, that was strange, all of us missing our alarm call. Brad was livid with Rick. It's such a sneaky thing to do, but that was just the kind of guy he was. Brad reckons Rick put something in our coffee so we'd sleep in and miss the sunrise. I wasn't fussed – seen one sunrise seen them all – but, yeah, Brad was furious.'

'Furious enough to hurt him?'

'Well, no, of course not. I didn't mean...'

Rosie saw the colour rush to Emma's cheeks so she hurried on before Emma had a change of heart about being so chatty.

'How long have you known Rick?'

'Let me think. I joined the Myth Seekers Society at the beginning of the year. I met Rick there, and Brad, Phil and few of the others. Boy, some of those guys were dull – a bit odd even – and all of them were completely focused on their obsession with chasing myths and legends. Someone had to drop out of the trip to Marrakesh at the last minute so I was offered their place. It was a free holiday. I wasn't going to say no, was I?'

'So you got to know Rick better when you took trips abroad together? What about his wife, Helen?'

'I didn't get to know him well. I was the only girl in the group on the Morocco trip, and on the trip to Athens. I met Helen and Steph for the first time this weekend.'

'How did Rick treat you as a newbie and the only woman?'

'He was always okay with me. I tried not to spend a lot of time with him, or with Phil and his mates, for that matter. They're all old enough to be my father. Why Brad keeps going to the meetings is beyond me. When we were in Morocco we'd have breakfast together as a group, then when they set off on their scheduled activities, me and Brad would sneak off and go camel racing, dune surfing or take a jeep safari into the Sahara Desert – African extreme sports are an awesome buzz!'

'And it must have been amazing to visit Athens? Did you do any sightseeing there?'

'Yes, we did a bit of trailing around the ancient monuments. Brad insisted, actually. He said we couldn't come to the seat of modern democracy without spending some time soaking up the vibes of those who'd trodden the ground before us, or some such garbage.'

Rosie noticed Emma couldn't meet her eyes and she made a note to mention it to Matt later. Was she embarrassed because her boyfriend was interested in early Greek civilization or was it something else?

Emma laughed. 'I know, I know, I'm sorry. My boyfriend is a nerd. All this myth stuff – treasure hunting, following ancient maps and setting out on quests – it's just, well, it's just so pointless. Why waste your time doing all that when you could be water-skiing on the Aegean Sea or abseiling down the rock face of the Corinth Canal?'

'So you don't have any idea why anyone would want to shoot Rick?'

'Well, you and Mia were there, you saw how he went on. Rick's always been a bit, well, a bit disrespectful to Phil and a few of the other long-standing members who were fixtures at the club before he arrived. It was like he wanted them to leave so he could take over and start afresh. He was an obnoxious moron to everyone at one time or another, even Brad. For instance, Phil's writing this book on the myths of Europe or something, right? Well, Rick was always taking the p... Well, ridiculing him at every opportunity. Phil self-published his last book because he couldn't get a publisher interested. After Rick mentioned it, I thought I'd look the book up on Amazon. It's got a few reviews – probably from his anoraky friends – but there's one review that is blisteringly awful and guess who wrote it? Rick! Now, if *I* was so obsessed with a subject that I'd spent years and years writing a book about it, I certainly wouldn't have been happy if I got a one star review from the chairman of my local club. If you ask me, I reckon it was Phil who shot Rick.'

'For writing a bad review?' scoffed Rosie.

'People have been murdered for less! Right, I think I'll persuade Brad to go for a drink at the Drunken Duck. Hey, Matt, if it's okay with you, once this is all sorted, I'd love to do the assault course at Ultimate Adventures, that way this whole week in the wilds of Willerby wouldn't have been a *total* waste of time.'

'No problem.'

Emma stood up, maintaining eye contact with Matt, a slight

smile parting her lips. She straightened her spine and elongated her slender arms above her head in a felinesque stretch causing the shape of her pert breasts to protrude from her skin-tight gym top. Rosie took in her pixie-like features; the upturned nose, her neat mouth devoid of enhancement as she had no need for cosmetics to augment her natural attractiveness. She did wonder why Emma had chosen to dye her hair a non-descript auburn colour when her eyebrows and lashes indicated her natural colouring was a vibrant copper which would have complimented her colouring so much better. Clearly she did still harbour a little vanity despite constantly professing to be a tomboy.

'Bye everyone!'

Chapter 15

'Well?' asked Matt when Emma had driven off in Brad's car that was more rust than bucket.

'Well, what?'

'This is usually the point at which you say "it's Emma" or "it's Brad".'

'No I don't!'

'Yes you do. You always think it's the person we've just talked to. And I definitely thought you would try to squeeze what Emma has just told us into one of your outlandish theories as to why she could be the only person responsible.'

'Well, I...'

Matt laughed and her cheeks coloured because that was exactly what she had been about to say, but having had a few minutes to think about it, she just couldn't see Emma, or Brad for that matter, wanting to shoot Rick, mainly because they both knew they were onto a good thing having Rick finance their trips abroad. Why would they want to put a stop to that? Rick had plenty of money; if he was willing to spend some of it on the club members so they could under-take foreign excursions together as a group then that was his prerogative. She couldn't blame Emma, or Brad – who probably didn't earn a huge salary either – for taking him up on his offer.

And could Emma really be responsible for stabbing her faithful bear Mitzy with an arrow? It didn't seem likely, but then who went around doing that sort of thing anyway? Ergh. Rosie's head felt like a marshmallow army had invaded and were partaking in a foam party, but there was no time to linger on her misfortune because a police car was winding its way down the drive towards the Windmill Café.

After spending the best part of an hour giving a statement to a police constable who took the ancient art of pedantry to a whole new level, Rosie watched him place poor Mitzy in a plastic evidence bag. Feeling like a toddler whose favourite toy had been confiscated for a misdemeanour she hadn't committed, she made the hooded-eyed officer promise to keep her informed of when she could have him back. She saw the look of disbelief on the man's face, but he wasn't the sort of person who would understand that the bear was the only item she possessed that had belonged to her father and precious memories were tied up in his threadbare fur.

She showed him out through the French doors and they both paused on the terrace whilst they waited for Matt to finish scrolling through his mobile phone before shaking the officer's hand.

'What are you looking at?' asked Rosie.

Instead of answering her question, Matt turned to the policeman. 'I've just read on the Willerby Gazette's website that the police have concluded their search of the area surrounding Garside Priory and they found a chisel hidden under a rock close to where we camped for the night. Why didn't you mention it?'

'I wasn't sure whether that information was going to be released,' sniffed the man, rolling his eyes at Matt's impertinence for questioning the police's procedures and their unwillingness to share their discoveries with the public.

Rosie leaned over Matt's shoulder to take a closer look at the write-up by intrepid journalist, Dan Forrester. A swirl of citrusy cologne sent a frisson of desire snaking around her abdomen and it took her a few seconds to drag her thoughts back to the subject at hand.

'A chisel, though? Not a quiver filled with poisoned arrows, or a long bow, or a recurve bow or ... what's the other type of bow called?'

'Composite. So, do the police think the chisel is connected to what happened to Rick Forster?' pressed Matt.

'I'm not at liberty to say.'

'But Rick wasn't attacked with a chisel,' said Rosie, wrinkling her nose in confusion.

'True. Have the police made any further progress on locating the bow?'

'Perhaps you should direct your questions to Mr Forrester. Good evening, Miss Barnes, Mr Wilson. If either of you think of anything else that might assist with our enquiries, then please do contact us. Otherwise, try not to worry, we have everything under control.'

'Unlikely,' muttered Matt as they watched the most

unfriendly police officer in Norfolk amble back to his car and sling Mitzy unceremoniously in the boot.

'I've had an idea,' said Rosie, her eyes still following the red taillights of the police vehicle wind through the country lanes. 'Why don't you give your farmer friend a call and see if he knows anything about the chisel?'

'Why?'

'Because if it was there before Sunday night, don't you think one of his dogs would have sniffed it out?'

'Maybe...'

'And the fact they didn't *could* mean someone brought it with them on our camping trip and maybe it's connected in some way to Rick's shooting.'

'I'm not sure about that, but I don't mind giving Giles a call.'

'Thanks, Matt.'

Matt meandered out to the terrace to make his call and Rosie returned to her kitchen to set the kettle to boil. A wave of sheer exhaustion gripped her bones and squeezed out whatever ounce of energy remained. Her brain tumbled with a kaleidoscope of ideas and counter-ideas, all searching for a ledge upon which to park their theories. Maybe she should have gone with Emma and Brad to drown her anxieties with a couple of the Drunken Duck's finest beverages.

'So, what did he say?'

'Giles has seen the Gazette piece, too, and he came to exactly the same conclusion as you. Well done, Sherlock.'

Rosie beamed and Matt rolled his eyes at her, but smiled as well.

'He said that he walks his dogs past the spot where the chisel was found every morning and every evening. He agrees with you – one of them would definitely have sniffed it out straight away but he's been avoiding the area where we camped since Rick was attacked for obvious reasons. So the chisel has to have been hidden by someone on Sunday night or Monday morning.'

'Why not just dropped accidentally?'

'Because it was found *underneath* a rock.'

'But hidden by whom?'

'Well, it can only be one of three people, can't it? Freddie and I don't carry that sort of equipment on wild camping trips, and I'm sure you're going to tell me that you and Mia don't own anything like a tatty old joiner's chisel.'

'No – whisks, spatulas and wooden spoons are the tools of *our* trade.'

Matt laughed. 'I'm surrounded by a bunch of complete obsessives – myth seekers, legend lovers, baking boffs, adrenalin junkies!'

'Oh, that's the pot calling the kettle! Talking of pots, I'm starving. Shall I cook something?'

'Unless you fancy indulging in some pub grub?'

Suddenly all Rosie wanted to do was escape the Windmill Café, to put the distressing incident out of her mind for a few hours and submerge herself in the rumble of conversation, the crackle of a log fire and a plate of Archie's hearty fayre.

'Thanks, Matt, I'd love that.'

She grabbed her pristine wax jacket and one of Georgina's hand-knitted scarves and followed Matt out to the car park.

She struggled to put words to the emotions swirling around her body as they made their way to the Drunken Duck where she suspected every one of the guests from the lodges would be eating that night. Perhaps a night with Matt and a takeaway in a wooden cabin huddled beneath the arboreal canopy would be a much more inviting prospect than having dinner with a group of people that possibly included a proficient marksman amongst its ranks – irrespective of the delicious food on offer.

Rosie's suspicions proved to be only partially correct. Phil, Steph and Helen were indeed at the pub but there was no sign of Emma and Brad. She assumed they had changed their mind and gone to the upmarket bistro in the next village so they could enjoy a more intimate dining experience.

For a few uncomfortable moments, the spectre of Rick's assailant lurked large in their company, but then everyone made a valiant effort to pretend nothing had happened. Phil regaled everyone with a detailed story about the group's trip to the Isle of Man and his continuing research for his next book. Apparently, he had hoped to have another chapter finished by the end of their week in Norfolk but, unsurprisingly, the literary muse had deserted him. Rosie chatted about her love of baking as they all savoured the flavours and textures of the food on offer at the Drunken Duck, which as she had predicted was delicious – she even devoured a generous wedge of chocolate fudge cake.

With everyone's stomachs replete, the prickly atmosphere of earlier morphed into mellowness and the conversation became less stilted, more jovial. For a couple of hours, Rosie managed to fool herself that things at the Windmill Café were normal; but the insidious coil of questions still needing answers eventually crept back in and she couldn't forget that once again she had involuntarily become embroiled in something disturbing. What with the poisoning in August and now this, she wondered if she should consider handing in her notice and moving on – even though neither incident had been her fault.

The very thought of leaving Willerby caused her stomach to flip-flop with distress. She loved everything about the village and the little Windmill Café which had woven its magic into her heart and she desperately wanted to stay. She thought of her approaching 'date' with Matt for Grace and Josh's Christmas wedding and enjoyed the sparkle of anticipation it caused in her chest. Seeing the couple together, happy, excited about starting their life together in the village they had grown up in, surrounded by friends and family – well, it made her think there might be an outside possibility she could find that too if she could only muster the courage to take a leap of faith into the dating game.

One thing she knew for sure was that she didn't want to be alone for ever. Before her father had passed away, her parents had enjoyed a strong, loving marriage filled with plenty of laughter, togetherness and mutual respect. Georgina might complain about Jack's obsession with music but Rosie knew she loved him fiercely. She wanted the same kind of relationship for herself. Just because she had made one disastrous choice with Harry didn't necessarily mean her next one would be.

Could she see herself dating Matt? Who was she kidding? Yes! He was extremely attractive with a surfer-dude thing going on, and, if the sparkle of desire she felt when he kissed her was anything to go by, she was certainly attracted to him. On top of that, he was intelligent, supportive and generous with his time, not to mention their shared love of puzzle solving.

But what did he think of her? Would the personality issues she still struggled to master be a barrier to a long-term liaison? Maybe. If she delved beneath the surface, their differences were stark. She was a neat freak, he was a clutterbug; she was organized and methodical, he was more intuitive in his thinking. He loved action-packed itineraries in the rugged outdoors; her idea of a good time was swinging in a hammock with a cocktail in one hand and a glossy cookery book in the other.

Or maybe there was something in the old adage that opposites attract? If so, perhaps they could look forward to a long and happy marriage! Oh, well, whichever way she looked at it, she was excited about being Matt's plus one for Grace and Josh's wedding and that told her all she needed to know. She had changed since she had first met Matt, Mia and Freddie six months ago. She hadn't said anything to anyone, but she'd been working hard on minimizing the clean gene she seemed to have involuntarily activated.

She knew she was a work in progress, but wasn't everyone?

At least her life now had a smoother cadence. She enjoyed her job as café and holiday site manager and appreciated the autonomy Graham gave her to run the business how she chose, using her own initiative instead of deferring to someone else because she lacked confidence in her skills. She loved her quirky new home and the Merlot-infused nights out with Mia, and now Grace, and couldn't believe she could boast to Georgina about taking part in a wild camping expedition, despite its disturbing outcome. All she had to do was solve the mystery of who shot Rick and life could return to normal.

Chapter 16

Rosie stared out of the window of her flat. The fields surrounding the windmill were flooded with ivory moonlight almost as bright as day. The arched canopy overhead was overcast and grey and provided the perfect backdrop for the swooping, squawking gang of crows that looked more like overgrown bats and instigated a curl of unease in her stomach. Matt had only dropped her off half an hour ago and had offered to sleep on one of the sofas either in her lounge or downstairs in the café. She regretted her refusal already. Whichever way she looked, north, south, east or west, the shadow-filled scene spread out before her had a malevolent feel.

She turned away, her gaze inevitably falling on her bedroom door. There was no way she could contemplate sleeping in there after the incident with the arrow. It was such a despicable thing to do to stab a child's soft toy like that! However, it meant that she and Matt must have rattled someone's cage with the direction of their questions, it was just she had no idea whose. She decided to curl up on the sofa with one of the peppermint and white cashmere throws Graham had brought back from Thailand. She began to relax, staring out at the starry sky, praying that sleep would ambush her before she resorted to the brandy.

Unfortunately, that night sleep played on the opposing team. Rosie glanced at her watch and was amazed to see it was only midnight. She groaned, giving herself a stern talking to about the safety of being upstairs in a windmill that had only one access route via a spiral staircase – through two sturdy *locked* doors. As she reached forward to switch off the lamp on the table beside her, she heard the crunch of footsteps on the gravel gate outside the window.

She sat bolt upright, her heart pounding so hard she thought it might actually escape from her ribcage. Tiny electric spasms of fear coursed through her veins and radiated out to her fingertips and for a moment she couldn't move. She just sat there, straining her ears, waiting for the next sound to send her imagination into the stratosphere. She thought she was going to have a coronary.

Oh God, was it her turn to be impaled by an arrow? Finally, her brain connected to its modem and she scrambled up from the sofa, grateful she hadn't undressed for her night on her temporary bed. She ran to the kitchen, mentally running through the available weapons at her disposal and deciding on a carving knife. She grabbed the largest from the wooden block, raising it high above her head in a dramatic fashion, and fixed her eyes on the door leading from the staircase - but nothing happened.

She crept towards the window overlooking the terrace, squinting down through the gloom, terrified about what she might see. Would it be an archer, the string of their bow primed and ready to release the arrow, its tip dipped in poison so that it would kill her instantly? However, she couldn't see anything and was in the process of persuading herself that she had been hearing things when there was a loud knock on the front door and she let out a terrified scream.

Still clutching the knife for dear life, she scrambled in her bag with her left hand, searching for her mobile to call the police. When eventually she pulled the phone from its slumber at the very bottom of her bag, it slithered from her fingers and fell to the floor. As she leaned down to collect it, there was another even louder knock. This time she paused and her sensible side poked its head above the parapet. What kind of attacker knocked on the door? Twice?

A confident one, or maybe one with nothing to lose!

She was about to dial 999 when a handful of stones rattled against the windowpane and she heard a cry from down below.

'Rosie? Are you awake?'

'Omigod, Matt!'

She rushed to the window and opened it, leaning forward so she could see him.

'What are you doing here? You scared me half to death!'

'Is that a kitchen knife in your hand?'

'Yes, it is.'

Rosie had forgotten she was still holding it. She briefly considered telling him she was slicing onions but she knew he wouldn't believe her and she would have to admit to her mistake of believing she would be fine staying at the flat by herself.

'Why?'

'Mitzy is skewered with an arrow and then I hear someone creeping around the windmill in the dark. What would *you* think?'

'Ah, yes. I get it. I should have called you from the car park. Do you think you could let me in? I think it could be minus ten out here and I forgot to put on my thermal underwear.'

Rosie smiled as a surge of warmth filtered through her veins. She had never been more pleased to see Matt lingering on her doorstep. She would definitely not be sending him home this time. She knew her limitations when it came to dealing with potential attackers.

'Erm, why are you here? Not that I'm complaining. I know I should have jumped at your offer to take the sofa. Turns out I'm a big fat coward!'

'No one can blame you – especially after the most recent development.'

'What recent development?'

'So you haven't seen the news?'

'No.'

'When I got home, Mum told me there had been a police announcement on the late bulletin about identifying the fingerprints found on the chisel, and after that I couldn't let you stay here by yourself, so I raced back like a knight-in-a-muddy-SUV in case you were scared.'

'I was scared, but it turned out to be your fault!'

Rosie rolled her eyes as she filled the kettle, the delayed reaction to the relief that her midnight intruder was Matt making her feel light-headed.

'So, come on, don't keep me in suspense. Whose fingerprints were they?'

'Brad Cookson's.'

'They found Brad Cookson's fingerprints on a chisel that was hidden under a rock next to our camp ground?' she gasped. 'That's ... well, that's...'

'I know. I couldn't get my head round it either.'

'At least it explains why he and Emma didn't come to the Drunken Duck last night. But what does it mean? Do the police think he shot Rick?'

'Before I came over here, I called DS Kirkham at Norfolk Constabulary. He was happy to talk to me because when they spoke to Brad he admitted the chisel was his straight away. He told them that he hadn't noticed it was missing, and it must have fallen out of his rucksack when he and Emma settled down for the night. The police are keeping an open mind, after all, Rick wasn't stabbed in the ankle, was he? So, we're back to square one, not to mention the fact that Ultimate Adventures was featured prominently in the news item! At this rate we'll be bankrupt before Christmas.'

'I'm sorry, Matt. Are you okay? You look ... well, you look exhausted.'

Matt rubbed the heels of his palms over his eyes and Rosie's heart gave a nip of sympathy. She handed him a cup of decaffeinated coffee and he offered her a weak smile of gratitude, his usual cheerful expression missing-in-action and replaced by a seriousness she had rarely glimpsed before.

Rosie hated seeing Matt like this and she was desperate to help, yet her own scattered thoughts bombarded her brain. There was something niggling at the back of her mind, some inconsistency that was just beyond reach. She knew that if she was going to solve the mystery of Rick's injury any time soon, she needed to think outside the self-imposed parameters of orderliness and indulge in a little creative thinking – that was what her father would have advised her to do if he'd been sitting next to her clutching his favourite Agatha Christie novel.

However, there was no way she could do that when her eyelids were drooping, so the most sensible thing to do was for them both to get some sleep and start again in the morning when they had more energy.

'Matt, I think we should get some rest and then go and talk to Brad and Emma ourselves in the morning.'

'Agreed, and anyway this coffee is disgusting.' Matt tried to produce a comedic grimace that didn't quite work, but some of his habitual chirpiness returned as he lay on the sofa opposite Rosie's, gave her a wink, and closed his eyes.

Rosie wrapped her throw around her body and spent a few moments studying her unexpected guest. She loved the way his eyelashes flickered against his cheeks, the slight twitch at the corners of his lips, and the slow rhythm of his breathing as sleep took him for its own. An unexpected mellowness descended over the room and erased the jagged edges of her anxiety. She wanted to stay awake all night to watch him sleep, to memorize every detail of Matt Wilson at rest so she could conjure up the image whenever she needed a smile. Sadly, her own cherubs of Morpheus had other ideas and she too was soon dreaming of happier times.

Chapter 17

As dawn dispatched fissures of apricot and salmon light through the leaden sky to the east, Rosie peeled open her eyelids. It took her a few seconds to remember that she had chosen to spend the night curled up on the sofa, but the change of scenery had meant her brain had worked out a plan whilst she slept. She rubbed her fists into her eye sockets and raked her fingers through her wayward curls, knowing she must look like she'd been dragged through the fields behind one of Farmer Giles' tractors.

With a quick glance in Matt's direction, she slipped from the room, showered, dressed and went down to the café where she spent the next hour whipping up a feast of breakfast muffins – two dozen with dried cherries, cranberries and cinnamon, two dozen with pumpkin and oats and a handful of toffee pieces, and two dozen with bran and prunes. The baking activity served to allay her nerves and the subsequent stint of extreme cleaning – during which she eradicated every tiny crumb – nudged her spirits even higher.

A delicious aroma rippled through the deserted room, tickling at her nostrils and she almost swooned. How she wished someone would bottle the fragrance of freshly baked cakes and distribute it to the needy. Coupled with freshly ground coffee and the offer of scrambled egg on toast, she hoped she wouldn't find it too difficult to lure her prey into the café so she could ask the questions she had finalized at 5 a.m. that morning.

She wrapped her old grey hoodie around her shoulders and sprinted to Brad and Emma's lodge, praying that Brad would answer her knock and not Emma. She hadn't been able to formulate a believable enough reason if Emma asked her why she'd chosen to invite Brad for breakfast and not her. Even to Rosie, it looked like a shaky excuse to get her clutches on the buttocks of steel that belonged to Brad Cookson. She had noted the excessive possessive streak that inhabited Emma's character and was loath to be the one to inflame her jealousy.

'Oh, hi Brad,' sighed Rosie, wisps of air lingering at her lips when she saw him crouched on his veranda busily untying the laces of his trainers. Clearly he'd been out for an early morning run to dispel the anxiety demons and she was a little surprised that Emma wasn't at his side. 'Erm, I've made some breakfast muffins if you fancy coming over to the café?'

'Sounds great. Emma's still asleep, though. We ... well, we both overindulged on the vodka last night and I think she came off worst.'

'Mmm,' Rosie said, averting her eyes from the closeness of the fit of his Lycra running shorts. She knew Brad had seen her because a flicker of a smirk flared in his eyes, the colour of liquid chocolate. He really did ooze sex appeal. Every muscle in his body had been honed to peak condition, not overblown from multiple sessions in the gym – just perfectly in proportion. A fleeting image of his naked torso floated across her mind and she felt a spasm of heat radiating from her chest to her face and she cringed.

'Okay, lead the way.' Brad grabbed his Gore-Tex cycling jacket and followed Rosie to the café. 'Do you need any help with the ... oh, hi, Matt. I didn't expect to see you here so early?' A knowing smile lingered on Brad's lips as his eyebrows shot into his forehead.

'How can anyone resist the smell of freshly ground coffee?'

'Exactly! It smells amazing, Rosie.'

Brad folded his six-foot-three frame into one of the café's white-washed wooden chairs and dug in to his plate of scrambled eggs, relishing every mouthful before sampling the pyramid of muffins.

'So, we heard on the news last night that the chisel the police found at the priory belonged to you,' began Rosie, conversationally.

She saw a shadow of panic flitter across Brad's handsome face, but he recovered well. She knew he would never be the sharpest tool in the box, but with Emma by his side, that area was amply covered. However, his girlfriend was tucked up in bed nursing a hangover and he had to fend for himself and if the tremble of his fingers on his mug was anything to go by his acting skills would win no awards.

'Yeah, I carry all sorts of useless stuff with me when we come on trips like this. I didn't even notice it was missing until they called me about it. It's not worth much but I'm glad to have it back.'

Brad's flippant response caused Rosie's conclusion over the discrepancy between his explanation and the evidence contained in Dan Forrester's article to crystallize. She levelled her gaze to his and he shifted uncomfortably in his chair, flicking his eyes towards the door.

'So, can you explain how a chisel can accidentally fall out of a rucksack and land *underneath* a rock?'

'I...'

Rosie scrolled through the Willerby Gazette's website until she arrived at the photograph accompanying the article and shoved her phone under Brad's nose.

'And if it didn't fall out, then you must have hidden it.'

'No, I...'

'Which means that you didn't want anyone to find it in your possession,' continued Matt, keen to ratchet up the pressure on Brad.

'Well, I...'

Beads of perspiration had started to collect at Brad's temples, his fidgeting was becoming more pronounced and he held his lower lip between his teeth to stop it from trembling.

'So, that leads us to assume that you could have hidden a few other belongings that you didn't want anyone to find.'

'No, I...'

'Like a quiver full of arrows and a recurve bow...'

'Hey, hey, now hang on. I...'

'Maybe it just started as a bit of a prank to frighten Rick, but unfortunately one of the arrows actually hit the target and you panicked.'

'I didn't...'

'And you had to get rid of the weapon quickly.'

'Or perhaps,' said Matt, snatching the deduction baton from Rosie. 'You were actually aiming for Rick's chest and missed?'

'Stop it! Stop it! I had nothing to do with Rick's injury! Nothing!'

'Well, we only have your word for that, don't we? And I might not be a seasoned detective, but it's not difficult to see that you're hiding something, Brad, and if that's the attempted murder of...'

'Attempted murder?'

Brad's mouth gaped open and he blanched. Every muscle in his body seemed to deflate like a pricked balloon and Rosie wondered why she had ever found him attractive. His jaw was too angular, his eyes had taken on a heavy, haunted expression and his pallor told her he used fake tan. The outward-bound daredevil had retreated into his protective shell.

'I did not ... I haven't...'

To Rosie's astonishment tears began to trickle down Brad's cheeks. She shot a glance at Matt whose expression displayed a hint of surprise too. She decided to switch tactics by scooting forward to the edge of her seat and offering Brad a smile of sympathy which only caused his face to crumple even more. He dropped his face into his hands and his body began to heave with silent sobs. He looked like a wounded animal, cornered, cowering and expecting the next blow to finish him off.

'Brad, I'm sorry about asking you all these questions, but after the piece on the news last night, Matt's business is facing ruin. All we want to do is find out who did this to Rick so that we can just get back to normal. If you know anything, anything at all, you have to tell us.'

Brad accepted the handful of tissues Rosie offered and worked hard to control his emotions. He inhaled a steadying breath and met Matt's eyes straight on, an expression of intense agony written boldly across his face.

'Okay. I'll explain. My brother died five years ago – cancer.'

A spasm of shock ricocheted through Rosie – those heart-breaking words had been the last thing she had expected Brad to utter. She watched him swallow down hard and a deter-mined expression replaced his tears.

'I'm ashamed to say I didn't cope very well with his death. I should have been there for my parents who were devastated beyond anything I've ever known, but instead I went off the rails. Oh, I didn't do anything illegal, not really. I thought that if I used up every ounce of energy, physically exhausting myself, my brain would be wiped clear of the never-ending trauma I couldn't get rid of any other way. So, I trained, and trained, and trained some more. It did help. I found that working out was a distraction from the constant agony of guilt; from the constant loop of questions that circled around my brain. Why had Karl died? How come I got to survive and not my brother? He was younger than me, only fifteen years old, for God's sake!'

Rosie reached across the table and squeezed Brad's hand, her own emotions churning as she fought to supress her memories of the same feelings of loss, bereavement, guilt.

'I became an adrenalin junkie, an extreme risk-taker. It was as though I was goading some invisible force to come and take me too. After a couple of years, it became an obsession. I *had* to run in every marathon going, *had* to join as many Three Peaks challenges as I could, *had* to cycle the Pennine Way, *had* to jump out of a plane. I'd have taken up sky-diving as a hobby if I could have afforded it. Yet here I am, still fit and healthy. Not even a sprained ankle. I'm ashamed to say that I even wished it had been me who got that arrow in my foot!'

Brad let out a sigh of disgust at his good fortune – as if he didn't deserve it.

'All these activities and expeditions were expensive. Much more than I could fund out of my salary. I couldn't go to Mum and Dad to ask for money. I didn't want them to know about what I'd become or the reasons behind it.'

Brad paused to blow his nose and to steady his voice. His demeanour had calmed but the haunted expression deep within his eyes was clearly evident. Rosie wondered why she hadn't noticed it before, but perhaps she had and hadn't wanted to dissect what it meant for fear of giving a platform to her own demons. Her heart ached for what Brad and his family had been through, were still going through probably, just like she and her family were.

'And the Myth Seekers Society?' Matt urged him gently.

'I had joined a couple of months before Karl passed away. The guys were so supportive when it happened. If it hadn't been for them ... well ... Anyway, when Rick joined and started to flash the cash I saw a way of satisfying my craving for more extreme challenges in more exotic places. Then I met Emma.

She showed up one night outside the club. I couldn't believe a girl like her was into myths and legends, much less wanted to attend a club dedicated to them. I mean, what girl does? I thought she'd made a mistake and had intended to come to the Wednesday night yoga club, that she'd stay for one session and we'd never see her again. But she stuck around. She even seemed to relish the most obscure theories of folklore Phil and Rick and some of the others had researched. It was amazing. And when she agreed to go on a date with me, well, I couldn't believe my luck. I thought that at last something good had come into my life.'

'And she went on one of the trips organized by the club?'

'Yes, someone had to drop out of the trip to Morocco and she leapt at the chance to take their place. We really got the chance to connect, and it turned out she was even fitter than me. Of course, she works in a gym so that's no surprise, but she's done the Three Peaks challenge loads of times and the London and Edinburgh marathons. We did a couple of charity half marathons together in support of Cancer Research UK before we went to Marrakesh.'

'What I don't understand is what you were doing with a chisel for the trek to the priory?'

Colour flooded Brad's cheeks and he averted his eyes. 'The trips, the marathons, the sky-diving, it was all becoming expensive – especially with Emma on board. Rick did subsidize our trips but there were still personal expenses to pay for, so I tried to help her out as much as I could and I had to get the cash from somewhere.'

'And...' urged Matt, earning himself an eye roll from Rosie.

She thought it was best to let Brad tell his story at his own pace, not to rush him to the conclusion which risked him missing something out that could be enlightening.

'Well, I'm not proud of what I did.'

'What did you do?'

'It started as a sort of dare at first, really. Last March, the Myth Seekers went up to Holy Island off the Northumberland coast. I wanted a souvenir of my trip so I helped myself to a chunk of the Lindisfarne Castle. I didn't think too much of it at the time but when I got back I was in one of the internet chat rooms us myth seekers frequent and I showed a photo of it to one of the guys from the US. He offered me a hundred quid for it. I was astounded and snatched his hand off. I mean, a hundred quid?'

Brad ran his fingertips through his cropped hair, his eyes flicking between Rosie and Matt, his expression filled with shame, yet pleading for understanding at the same time. Whilst Matt's face remained stern, Rosie gave a slight nod of acknowledgment so that Brad would continue with his confession.

'That started me thinking. If I could collect a little piece of history from all our trips, home and abroad, maybe I could make a bit of extra money for me and Emma. Easy. I didn't think of the legalities. I mean, Marrakesh is littered with discarded artefacts. Who would mind? So I brought back a small piece of mosaic and flogged it on the internet; made some cash again.'

'Did Emma know what you were doing?'

'Yes, I'm not good at keeping secrets. She thought it was a

great way to supplement our funds. But when she suggested we did that statue in the museum in Athens, well, that got me wondering if we might have gone just a bit too far. So I decided I'd lay off for a while, but when we got back to the hotel, Rick was waiting for us. He ordered us to turn out our bags and our pockets, and when we did he went mental.

'I thought he was going to have a coronary right there in front of us. He went on and on about priceless relics, irreplaceable artwork, stuff like that. At the next Myth Seekers meeting after we returned home he pulled me to one side and told me that if he saw anything else posted on the internet for sale he would involve the police. I didn't want to sell the stuff after that, but, well, Emma said we already had it and we should just get rid of it, and then call it a day. So I did and Rick found out. He was even angrier this time. I don't blame him. I shouldn't have listened to Emma. I knew it was wrong.'

'So Rick was going to report you to the police?'

'Yes. I apologized. I confided in him about my addiction to adrenalin surges and other extreme risk-taking behaviour since the death of my brother. I promised to get some counselling and in return he said he'd think about whether to report me over the course of this week. He seemed sympathetic. I hoped ... well...'

'And yet you had a chisel with you when you went up to the priory? Did you intend to chisel off a souvenir of your visit there too?' Matt asked, his jaw working hard at remaining still.

Brad swallowed down hard again and tears gathered along

his lower lashes whilst he scrutinized his fingernails. Rosie held her breath, praying he was about to deny any more involvement.

'Yes. I'm ashamed to say that's exactly what I intended to do. But when I saw Rick lying there with an arrow sticking out of his ankle I panicked. I wanted to get rid of the chisel before anyone could search me. I'm so sorry. I shouldn't have done any of it. I just needed the money. It's no excuse for what I've done, but it's the truth. I'm terrified Rick's going to inform the other members and they expel me from the group. But whatever happens to me, you have to believe me, I did not shoot him with that arrow.'

As Brad crumbled for a second time, Rosie felt a surge of sympathy. Sitting there at the table, wiping his cheeks on his sleeve, he looked like a desolate puppy threatened with being left out in the rain after a misdemeanour. Her instinct told her he wasn't the culprit, but she had to reach her conclusions using logic, not instinct, and it did look like all the evidence pointed to the undeniable fact that Brad had a strong motive for wanting Rick out of the way. Quite apart from Rick's threat to go to the police, the Myth Seekers had become a surrogate family to Brad and the risk of being excluded from their meetings would have had a devastating impact on his life, especially if Emma continued to attend without him.

Rosie poured Brad another cup of tea, added a heaped teaspoon of sugar, and he sipped it gratefully. 'Brad, the night of the wild camping, did you notice anything unusual? Anything at all?'

'No, I don't think so. Emma and I went with Rick to collect

water from the stream for our evening brew, then we huddled together in our sleeping bags. We knew we had to be up early for the trek over to the priory before sunrise. I slept surprisingly well, but Phil's already told me that was because Rick had put something in our coffee so we'd all miss the show. Rick was no angel either, Rosie.'

'So we are finding out.'

'I think I should be getting back to the lodge before Emma freaks out and thinks I've been shot by a random archer, too. Thanks for the breakfast, Rosie, and I'm sorry about ... well, about the, you know, the crying.'

'You're welcome, and don't worry about it, Brad. I've lost someone close to me too and I understand how emotions can just ambush you at the most inopportune of times.'

Rosie watched Brad walk back to his lodge, his hands shoved deep into his pockets, elbows flapping, head bowed, and her heart softened further. The sudden death of a loved one changed a person for ever, sometime for the better, sometimes not, but nevertheless, you were never the same person you were before. You struggled to make sense of your new world with a huge void at its centre.

'You know, I thought we were getting better at this mystery-solving stuff,' groaned Matt. 'But I feel like we're going around in circles. I need to get out of here. Fancy a walk over to Willerby? I could do with the exercise. We can call in at Adriano's Deli for an espresso and a couple of their delicious cannoli to sustain us on the walk back?'

Rosie hesitated. She should really stay at the Windmill Café and wait for Mia to arrive for another morning of Hallowe'en-inspired baking. They still had the pistachio macaron frogs and the cheese straw twisted fingers to triple-test before the party on Friday, as well as a run through with the spicy pumpkin punch and the chocolate Matchmaker spiders Mia had been working on. On the other hand, she wanted to help Matt comb through all the information they had gathered over the last two days.

Matt was right, every single one of the five suspects staying at the Windmill holiday site had a motive, as well as the opportunity to shoot Rick whilst he relaxed in the cloister of Garside Priory enjoying the solitary pleasure of watching the sun rise through the archway. However, within moments, the pendulum of doubt swung back the other way and she was forced to conclude that, in her opinion, none of them were really capable of perpetrating such a vicious deed, even to someone as unpopular as Rick.

'Count me in. I'll just leave some instructions for Mia.'

Chapter 18

Rosie dashed across the terrace outside the Windmill Café and made her way to the car park where Matt was waiting for her for their one-mile walk to Willerby. She was greeted by an insistent breeze, edged with a suspicion of ice that nipped her extremities and made her wish she'd grabbed her gloves. She needn't have worried because Matt slotted his warm palm into hers and gave it a squeeze, sending sparks of heat through her veins and a curl of pleasure to her lips.

As the carpet of russet and orange leaves attested, winter was definitely on its way, but it hadn't quite reached its destination and the air smelled of damp soil and wood smoke from the fires and log burners in the village. It didn't take long for the brisk exercise to work its magic and clear Rosie's muddled thoughts. In other circumstances, she would have thoroughly enjoyed the romantic walk through the countryside, hand-in-hand with Matt Wilson, the most gorgeous guy in Willerby!

That morning the village was wearing its best outfit; each tree, hedgerow, bush and lawn draped with shafts of sunshine which gave the whole scene a sepia-tinted hue. The main street, which wound leisurely towards the church at the far end, was as bright and cheerful as its reputation.

Adriano's crouched at the opposite end of the road to the Drunken Duck and since the deli's arrival two years ago, it had become an institution in the village. It was the sort of place that brought a smile to your face simply by looking at its welcoming exterior; a bow-fronted window stretched across the whole façade like a wide grin, a front door painted in a cheery scarlet and a necklace of bunting in the colours of the Italian flag.

Matt pushed open the door and the tinkle of a brass bell overhead announced their arrival. Rosie paused on the threshold for a second, bracing herself for the visual onslaught of all things Italian, from dangling salamis and round fat mozzarella cheeses to freshly baked *crostata di frutta* filled with apricots, cherries, peaches and nectarines, and cream-filled cannoli. Rosie could already feel her taste buds zinging in anticipation. Everything in the deli spoke of the warmth and friendship of a treasured Italian friend who, no matter how long it had been between visits, it still felt like you had last seen them the day before.

Matt ordered a double espresso and grabbed a seat at the table next to the window. Rosie loitered at the glass display cabinet, unable to choose between a slice of tiramisu layer cake or ricotta and crushed pistachio pie until she heard Matt's phone buzzing and made a snap decision to try one of the cannoli.

'Hi, Freddie.'

Matt's eyes rested on hers whilst he listened intently to

what his friend and colleague had to say, which culminated in a broad grin.

'Freddie, you're an absolute genius. Why didn't I think of that? Are you going over there now? Okay, let me know if you find anything?'

'What was all that about?' asked Rosie, depositing three dessert plates on the table and taking a seat opposite him.

'Freddie has a couple of friends who are keen detectorists. They're on their way over to the woodland where we camped out on Sunday night and they're going to follow the path we took to the Priory to see if they can uncover anything. You never know, maybe they'll get lucky and find a discarded bow and quiver full of arrows. I know it's a long shot, but it's worth a try, don't you think?'

'Inspired!' laughed Rosie, nibbling at her cannoli and holding her hand under her chin to catch any flaky pastry crumbs, picking them up with the tip of her tongue. 'So, what do you...'

'Hi! You must be Rosie Barnes from the Windmill Café. Adriano waxes lyrical about your strawberry and kiwi tartlets, not to mention your fig and walnut scones and pineapple and coconut cookies. I told him that he should really be talking up our Tuscan delicacies, but he insists that "this town is big enough for the both of us",' giggled the young waitress, as she performed a passable imitation of her esteemed boss Adriano Danapo in the guise of a Mafia Godfather. 'Oh, I'm Corrine, by the way.'

'Hi Corrine, great to meet you. Have you just started working at Adriano's?' asked Rosie, taking in Corinne's graduated bob, the colour of liquid coal, and bright scarlet lipstick that matched her nose stud that twinkled in the deli's overhead lights.

'Yes, I've been here six weeks and it's absolutely the best job in the world!'

'I have to agree with you. Who wouldn't want to spend their working day in here surrounded by *Crema Fritta*, *Cartellate*, *Zeppole* and *Cassatedde*? Delicious!'

'Well, I'm sure they are, but sadly I can't eat any of them.'

'Why not?

'I'm gluten-intolerant.'

'Really? What a shame,' said Matt, raising his eyebrows at Rosie when Corinne wasn't looking. 'So, do you just stick to the *zabaglione* and chocolate *panne cotta* then?'

'I wish. I'm actually allergic to chocolate.'

'Really? That must cancel out pretty much every dessert in the place. I suppose you can always indulge in the wonderful antipasti.'

'Not all of it.'

Rosie knew she shouldn't really ask her next question, but she did anyway. 'Why not?'

'I'm vegetarian.'

She heard Matt try to make a snigger sound like a cough and she didn't dare catch his eye for fear she would crumple into laughter and offend their new friend with the sing-song Welsh accent who had chosen to work in a café where she couldn't eat any of the food.

'Well, welcome to Willerby, Corinne. I hope you'll be as happy here as I am.'

'I absolutely know I will. The best thing about it is being so close to the sea. I adore every water sport going and yesterday I met a guy called Freddie who offered to take me windsurfing! He even said he would show me a place where you can go wild swimming! Awesome!'

A shiver shot down Rosie's spine. There was nothing she would like less than spending an afternoon swimming in one of the rivers or canals scattered around the Norfolk country-side for fun, even in Freddie's exuberant company.

'Perhaps you could invite Rosie along?' suggested Matt, a smirk playing around the corners of his mouth causing tiny matching dimples to appear and Rosie's stomach gave a pleasurable lurch. She rolled her eyes at him and decided not to grace his comment with a reply.

'I'd love you to join us, Rosie. I'll give you a call. Anyway, enough of my chatter, I'll let you two have some privacy,' grinned Corinne, clearly jumping to the wrong conclusion.

'Oh, no, we're not...' began Rosie, but Corinne had floated off to bombard other customers with a list of her allergies and her views on water sports, leaving behind a trail of jasmine perfume. Rosie crammed the last of her apple and caramel cannoli into her mouth, giving Matt a comedic look as her cheeks bulged like a food-hoarding hamster, before saying, 'Okay, let's talk through what we know about Rick's shooting.'

Matt's mood changed. He scratched at the smattering of blond stubble on his jaw before leaning back in his chair, crossing his boot over his thigh and expelling a long sigh of frustration.

'Rosie, I know we solved the last mystery before the police

did, but that doesn't mean we're going to do the same this time. I'm really worried about the business, I have to admit. Even if the mystery is cleared up by the weekend, we've just had another three cancellations for the week after next. That leaves us with only two groups for the assault course and both of them are from outside the area and probably haven't heard about what happened at Garside Priory yet. I've completely destroyed the business my father spent years building; not only that but the scandal is bound to have an impact on his name.'

The look of desperation on Matt's face made Rosie want to grab hold of him pull him into a hug, and the only thing stopping her was the knowing looks she was getting from Corinne. She experienced an overwhelming desire to apply every little grey cell at her disposal to uncover the perpetrator of the surprise assault on Rick, if only so that Matt's outward-bound centre would survive to offer the inhabitants of Norfolk the opportunity to fling themselves from the treetops or drag themselves through mud as part of so-called team building exercises for years to come. She couldn't bear for the place to close because of an unwarranted slur on its reputation.

After Matt had told her about his father's climbing accident, Rosie had googled the details. What Matt hadn't told her was how well-known Malcom Wilson had been in mountaineering circles and how his death had affected the whole community. Matt had been twenty-one and had just graduated from university and was about to take up a place at the police college in Hendon when the accident happened. His younger brother had finished his A levels and was heading to university so it was down to Matt to continue with the running of Ultimate Adventures in his father's absence. Far from feeling cheated, Matt had confided in her that he loved the outdoors lifestyle and he suspected he would have grown to hate being cooped up in an office, but that didn't prevent him from continuing his fascination with puzzles of every kind – including the assault courses he had built around the Ultimate Adventures woodland.

'Why don't we go over everything we know?' said Rosie, hoping something new would come of the exercise.

'If you think it'll do any good,' mumbled Matt, scrutinizing the contents of his espresso cup as if they were laced with poison.

Rosie ignored his lacklustre response and breezed forward in her deductions.

'Let's start with Helen who we know is having an affair with one of Rick's colleagues. Either separately or together, they could have driven over to Garside, laid low until the morning and then shot Rick when he arrived at the Priory. As far as motive is concerned, if they intended to kill Rick rather than just hurt him, then not only would Helen stand to inherit a sizeable sum, she wouldn't have to fight her way through the divorce courts. We also should factor in Rick's refusal to contemplate having a family. Remember, when we spoke to Helen she told us she couldn't forgive him for not telling her before they got married. That's a pretty tough situation to accept without a fight, don't you think? With Rick out of the way, she would be free, wealthy and have the chance of becoming a mother before it's too late.'

She waited until her attempt at amateur psychology had had the chance to seep under Matt's armour of realism. As she studied his face and the way his shoulders slumped, she was shocked to see he wore an air of defeat. He hadn't touched his espresso and his eyes were ringed with tiredness as he replied.

'But there's no evidence to suggest she was anywhere near the Garside Priory that morning. No one has come forward to say they saw a red Porsche, or a white Audi TT, screaming away from the scene – neither of them are the type of vehicle that would blend into the countryside. I've spent some time stalking every member of the group on social media and all Helen seems to do is go to the gym, have lunch with her friends, or organize the occasional charity dinner for Rick's accountancy company. And Tim Latimer is even wealthier than Rick, so I don't think either of them are interested in getting rid of him for his money. Sorry, Rosie, I know you're trying to help, but I don't think it's either of them.'

Undeterred, Rosie flicked through her internal Rolodex until she arrived at her next target.

'Okay, let's move on to Phil and Steph Brown. Rick found out about the two unauthorized withdrawals in the Myth Seekers Society's accounts and threatened to report Phil to the police for theft. Phil admits he withdrew the funds without the permission of the committee, but if you want my opinion, I doubt the Greater Manchester police would have taken the report too seriously, especially as the money was spent on a plaque to commemorate the Society's twentieth anniversary, not for his own use.'

'I agree with you,' said Matt, his chin starting to lift as his interest in her deductions sharpened. 'But let's not forget that Rick was constantly on Phil's case about something or other. We both saw how he went on at the camp. Perhaps Phil had just had enough of being bullied and snapped. It happens.'

'Yes, it happens, but I can't see Phil in a pair of green tights prancing through the fields with a bow and arrow slung over his shoulder. He doesn't look strong enough to even carry one as far as the priory without needing a sit down to get his breath back. And his eyesight is dreadful which is bound to effect his aim.'

'What about Steph? She's a bit more feisty, especially when it comes to protecting her husband.'

'Possibly.'

'And neither of them has an alibi. Phil was with us at the camp but we were all out of it. He could have laced our coffee, then pretended to be asleep and followed Rick up to the priory. Maybe when he realized what Rick was up to he just saw red? And Steph could have waited until Helen left for her assignation with Tim Latimer, then driven over to the site in their Volvo, shot Rick, hidden the bow and got back to the lodge before Helen came back.'

'A bit flimsy, though, isn't it?'

'Okay. What about Brad? He has plenty of motive. Rick knew about his sideline in selling valuable artefacts. I reckon the police would have definitely taken that seriously. It would be easy enough for them to gather the evidence they need for a prosecution from his internet accounts. He'd be looking at a hefty fine at the very least, and even if Rick relented about involving the police he wouldn't have been able to resist telling everyone at the Myth Seekers Society about what Brad had been up to. That club means the world to Brad – he would have been devastated if they'd voted to expel him.'

'Yes, I agree Brad has a strong motive. What he did has the most serious consequences. But I can't get away from the fact that he is still grieving over the death of his brother. And do you think he has the brains to come up with a plot to shoot Rick with an arrow just to shut him up? What about Emma? I have to admit she's at the bottom of my list. She hardly knew Rick and he wasn't threatening her with any kind of exposure as far as we know nor had he included her in his bullying regime.'

'You're right. I can't think of a motive unless she was upset about the way Rick was treating Brad, but they'd only been together for a few months. I think we can rule Emma out. Although, like Brad, she had the same opportunity to slip everyone a sedative and follow Rick to the priory, shoot him and then double back to make it look like she'd woken up with the rest of us. However, I reckon it was Rick that doctored everyone's coffee. Did you notice anyone refusing a drink?'

'No, sorry. I thought we all drank it.' Rosie paused, unsure whether she should say what had been coiling round her mind for a while. Oh, well, why not! 'What about a jealous former lover? We know Rick's been married twice before. Or an abandoned love child? Or a deranged stalker? Or perhaps someone whose business Rick liquidated?'

'Really, a deranged stalker? You're joking, right?'

'Sorry.'

Matt dropped his head into his palms and groaned. After a few minutes he raised his eyes and studied Rosie as she flicked through the notes she had scribbled on a napkin.

'What are our final conclusions then, PI Barnes? All the suspects on our list have a motive, all had opportunity, but it's unlikely that any of them would choose a bow and arrow as their weapon of choice.'

'I suppose one of them could have taken up archery in secret?'

'True. So again, they *all* could have done it.'

'It does seem that way.'

'Can I get you any more coffee?' asked Corinne, sensing a lull in their conversation.

'I think I've had enough coffee to last me a month!' declared Matt, swallowing his espresso in one go.

'Coffee, that's it!' cried Rosie. 'Why didn't I think of that sooner!?'

'What are you talking about?'

'Well, instead of wondering who put that sedative in our coffee, why don't we just ask Rick straight out whether or not it was him? He's the only one we haven't talked to and he should be out of surgery by now.'

'You know he refuses to take my calls. I must have tried a dozen times, and don't forget his threat of legal action!'

'I don't think his solicitor will have driven down from Manchester to visit him in hospital, do you? And Rick's used to being busy so I reckon he'll be going stir crazy about being confined to a bed not knowing anything about what's going on. So, instead of trying to ring him, why don't we drive over to the hospital where we can look him in the eye and tell him we know it was him who spiked everyone's drinks and see how he reacts?'

'It's an inspired plan! Come on, what are we waiting for?' cried Matt, jumping up from the table and rushing out of the café leaving her to pay the bill.

Chapter 19

The hospital car park was crammed to bursting and disgruntled would-be visitors circled the roads like predatory cats waiting to pounce on innocent mice.

'Look, there's a space!' declared Rosie.

There followed an almost comedic dash for the parking bay around the one-way system, which she was thankful they won, but as they drew into the space a wave of guilt hit her. What if the driver of the silver Saab's need was greater than their own? She craned her head over her shoulder to see with relief that the Saab had pulled into a space next to the pay meter.

'Good God! You need to take out a mortgage to pay the parking fees!' groaned Matt, reaching into his pocket for a handful of change.

'Have you worked out what we're going to say to Rick?' asked Rosie as they made their way towards the reception area where they had arranged, via a sympathetic Helen, to meet Rick.

'Not really. Let's just see how it goes, shall we? Bearing in mind the contents of his last text, I was surprised Rick agreed to talk to us at all, especially in person.'

'It's probably testament to the boredom of being stuck in hospital.'

A coil of trepidation had begun its insidious journey around Rosie's abdomen. As with many people, hospitals held painful memories, and this would be the first time she had set foot in one of their neon-bright corridors since she had lost her beloved father over twelve years ago. Her breath felt laboured from the concrete heavy block weighing down on her chest, and her head was stuffed with cotton wool, yet she knew she had to call on her reserves of courage to solve the mystery of Rick's shooting and rescue Matt's business. Anyway, she told herself sternly, other visitors to the hospital had far worse interviews to attend.

They had just stepped into the building when Matt's phone buzzed.

'Are you going to answer it?'

'No, look, there's Rick.'

'I think you should at least see who's calling.'

Matt extracted his phone and sighed. 'It's Freddie.'

'Talk to him. It might be important.'

'Hi, Fred.'

Matt's eyes lingered on Rosie as he listened to Freddie's report.

'That's great news, Freddie. Thanks for letting us know. I'm at the hospital with Rosie, visiting Rick, so I'll pass the information on to them both. Catch you later.' Matt slid his mobile into the back pocket of his jeans and met Rosie's eyes, a hint of excitement ignited in their depths. 'Would you believe the detectorists have found the riser and the limbs of the recurve bow used to shoot Rick? Both were discovered in a hollowed out oak tree in the woodland surrounding the Garside Priory. The police are testing them for fingerprints, but I doubt they'll find any.'

'You know, something else has just occurred to me...'

'Matt! Rosie! You're late. I've been sat here like an idiot for the last twenty minutes which means the coffees are on you!'

Rick spun his wheelchair towards the vending machine at speed, scattering a mother and toddler and an old man with a Zimmer frame from his path – he might have broken his ankle, but his pompous personality remained intact. Rosie rolled her eyes at Matt behind Rick's back and went to buy them all a coffee while Matt found a quiet corner to have a chat.

'Thanks for agreeing to talk to us, Rick. Rosie and I are as anxious as you are to get to the bottom of what happened.'

'Well, there's nothing else to do in this place except stare at a television screen. The doc refuses to discharge me until tomorrow at the earliest. I'd discharge myself, but that would probably affect any potential negligence claim.'

Rosie handed Rick a coffee, briefly wondering if his attitude would improve if she poured the hot beverage in his lap. She had been prepared to put Rick's grumpy demeanour down to the fact he was in pain and had been through a traumatic experience that she wouldn't wish on anyone. However, he did little to ingratiate himself to the innocent onlooker. She wondered if he ever allowed anything pleasant to pass his lips. He might be generous with his cash, but he certainly wasn't very charitable with his words.

'So, don't just sit there gawping like a pair of goldfish, what did you want to ask me?'

Rosie stared at Matt, signalling that she wanted him to take the lead. She was irritated with herself but she had completely lost her nerve. It wasn't just Rick's belligerent attitude; the waiting room they were sitting in was almost identical to the one she had visited many years before – the same plastic seats, same linoleum floor, same dull walls, same stark overhead lighting, same smell. It was all she could do not to throw her hands in the air and run.

'Okay. We wanted to ask you how you felt when you woke up on Monday morning, before you set off on your solo hike to the priory.'

'How I felt? Well, my first thought was what a bunch of lightweights I had chosen to spend my time with – including the professionals.' Rick gave Matt a malicious look, almost goading him to retaliate and when he didn't, he continued. 'We were there to see the sunrise and if I was the only person organized enough to make sure I was there on time, then hard luck on everyone else. It wasn't my responsibility to wake everyone up like a mother hen. I intended to take a few fabulous photographs to show Phil, and maybe do a presentation when we got back to Manchester to the club members. To say I'm disappointed that didn't happen is an understatement.'

Rick shifted his weight in his wheelchair and Rosie wonder how Matt was able to remain so calm, especially after his next comment.

'I shall be requesting a full reimbursement of the cost of

the camping trip from Ultimate Adventures. I trust there will be no problem with that, Matt?'

'Of course not.'

'And I only agreed to meet you today so I could tell you myself that I've instructed my solicitor to instigate personal injury proceedings on my behalf. I trust you are well insured?'

'Ultimate Adventures holds all the appropriate certificates and insurances,' said Matt politely but Rosie could see he had started to grind his teeth in an effort to keep a lid on his emotions. 'Thank you for your candour. I will inform my insurance company to expect your correspondence.'

Rosie glanced from one man to the next, amazed that Matt was able to continue to sit next to the man who was clearly relishing every verbal dig. However, she also realized that Rick's attitude would make it easier for Matt to ask the difficult questions they wanted answers to.

'So, I take it you don't know anything about the sedative that was found in everyone's coffee – the reason you were the only one who was able to wake up on time?'

'Sedative? What do you mean? There was no sedative in my coffee.'

'Exactly.'

'Hang on! Are you accusing me of spiking everyone's drink?'

A dark crimson colour flooded Rick's face and Rosie could feel his growing fury at the insinuation that he had been responsible. She didn't have to be an expert in psychology to deduce that he was genuinely shocked at Matt's question.

'I'm not insinuating anything. I'm simply asking whether you were aware of the fact.'

'This slanderous accusation is just a way of diverting blame from the substandard organization of the wild camping expedition. I...' As Rosie watched on she could almost see the cogs turning behind Rick's eyes as his anger morphed into curiosity. 'Are you telling me that someone drugged you?'

'Yes. Everyone on the trip felt groggy when they woke up apart from you.'

'So ... if that's true, it means this whole thing was organized days, maybe even weeks, in advance!'

'Exactly, and there's something else you might like to know. A recurve bow and a quiver full of arrows have been discovered hidden in a hollowed-out tree near our camp site which proves the shooting was pre-meditated and that you were the intended victim.'

'I really think the police should have called me about this first! Why should I have to learn about the discovery of the weapon that was used to shoot me from some random stranger?' Rick spluttered.

'I'm sure the police will contact you,' soothed Matt in his best conciliatory tone, ignoring the slur on his, albeit strained, relationship with Rick and choosing instead to focus on the questions they had come to ask, especially now they knew for sure that the drugging was linked to the shooting. 'Now that you know our coffee was spiked, do you still think the person responsible for all this is Phil?'

'No, I don't! That guy is totally useless, he couldn't organize a party in a winery, let alone plan a crime!'

'So, do you have any other suggestions?' urged Rosie, keen to exhaust their enquiries so they could leave the hospital.

Not only was a wave of nausea climbing through her chest, but she really didn't want to spend any longer than necessary in Rick's spiteful company.

'Well, much as it pains me to say this about people who are supposed to be my friends, I reckon it could be any one of them, apart from the fact that they're all cowards. But if I had to single one person out, then it would be Brad. I've uncovered some very disturbing information about the theft of ancient artefacts and if I wasn't incarcerated in this place, I would be demanding that the police arrest him immediately! In fact, have you finished with this ridiculous interrogation? Because if you have I'm going back to the ward to call them right now!'

Rick swivelled round in his wheelchair and glanced down the corridor that had emptied of patients and visitors.

'Where's Helen? Helen! Helen!'

'It's been good to talk to you, Rick,' said Rosie, as pleasantly as she could before linking her arm through Matt's and all but galloping from the hospital and back to where they had left the SUV. 'My God, Matt, broken ankle or not, I thought he was going to punch you at one point.'

'So did I. I have to admit that I have a boatload of sympathy for Phil and Brad having to share their club with a man like Rick Forster.'

'Me too! Not to mention how horrible it must be to be married to him! However, it looks like we're still searching for the person who put the sedative in our bedtime drinks on Sunday night – which leaves us with three possible suspects. I've also remembered something else we need to look into.'

213

Rosie hopped into the passenger seat and took out her phone, feeling one hundred per cent better now they had left the hospital and Rick's oppressive personality behind.

'I'm no expert, but whoever shot Rick managed to score a direct hit with their second arrow which means they must be a fairly accomplished archer.'

'I see where you're going! Archery is a regulated sport with formal rules and regulations and codes of conduct. Why don't you google every Archery GB registered club in the North West and make a few calls to see what you can find out about their membership whilst I drive us back to the windmill?'

Rosie spent the next hour trawling the internet, speaking to local archery club presidents, some more willing to chat to a potential new member than others. She managed to glean very little until she stumbled on a residential course run by a club in North Wales. The guy in charge regretted that he was unable to put her in touch with any fellow archers to regale her with all the fun times they had whilst shooting, but he did point her to a Facebook group with a public profile where their members posted photographs of competitions they took part in and the trophies they won for their respective clubs.

'Matt! Stop! You have to look at this!'

Matt pulled over to the side of the road and took Rosie's phone from her, his expression serious.

'My God, Rosie, I think you've cracked it! I think we need to talk to the police immediately.'

'There's just one more thing I need to do to confirm what I think could be the motive. I'll give my Uncle Martyn a call;

he has friends in a Manchester law firm who'll be able to take a quick trip to the Town Hall and we'll have the proof we need to bring this mystery to a conclusion.'

'I don't know about your childhood dream to train as a criminal defence solicitor, Rosie, but you'd make an amazing Crown prosecutor or private investigator. Maybe Freddie is right; perhaps we should set up a new business together – especially if Rick is still intent on closing me down even after we have delivered the person responsible.'

'I'm confident that once Rick hears what we've found out, the last thing on his mind will be pursuing a claim against Ultimate Adventures. Even the most comprehensive risk assessment couldn't contemplate the possibility of being shot by an arrow!'

'Thanks, Rosie. For saving my business, for everything. You are absolutely amazing!'

Rosie turned to Matt to offer a smile, but the intensity of his gaze whipped the air from her lungs. The atmosphere in the SUV was suddenly charged with electricity and her heart beat a cacophony of excitement and attraction against her ribcage. Her nerve endings tingled as she inched towards Matt, anticipating the sensation of feeling his lips on hers, his hands curled at her neck...

'God! Who's that!' grumbled Rosie, grabbing her phone and glancing at the caller ID. 'Oh, it's Uncle Martyn. He was always a quick worker – thank God!'

Rosie would always be grateful to her father's older brother who had come to their rescue when her mother had buried her head in the sand after her father's death. Her childhood home had been repossessed, but her uncle had managed to sort everything out, pay off their debts from the proceeds, and help them buy their cosy flat above a bakery.

'He's emailed the document through – and look, I was right!'

'We need to call the police right now. I'll ask DS Kirkham to meet us at the Windmill Café, and this time you can do the honours of explaining what we've discovered to everyone, Mademoiselle Poirot.'

Chapter 20

The next morning, all eyes rested on Rosie as she stood behind the marble counter in the Windmill Café, a place where she had often demonstrated the intricacies of her recipes. She wished that was what she was about to do now – showcase the best technique for producing a delicious Victoria sponge or a perfect apricot roulade, for her a much more inviting proposition than revealing the identity of the person who had shot Rick.

Swallowing down on her anxiety, she cast a quick glance around the gathering. Rick sat by the French doors in his wheelchair, like a king on a throne, his back straight, his leg elevated, a grim expression in his eyes. When DS Kirkham had arrived, Rick had vociferously insisted with his habitual arrogance that he should be furnished with the details surrounding his shooting, as well as the identity of the perpetrator, before everyone else. Rosie had to admit that he did have a point, until he'd continued with a demand that he should also be permitted to perform the role of raconteur himself and both demands had been promptly refused. At that moment, Rosie wished DS Kirkham had relented and Rick *was* standing in her shoes.

Helen sat in one of the white-washed chairs on the other side of the room, her ankles crossed daintily, steadfastly refusing to meet Rosie's eyes. When she had been told why they were congregating in the café, Helen had asked DS Kirkham if Tim Latimer could join them but he had refused her request. Without her friend by her side for support, she was clearly worried about what would happen when their relationship was disclosed to the group.

Phil huddled next to Steph on one of the leather sofas, holding onto her hand as if his life depended on it. The sunlight filtering through the window behind him made his sparse hair seem even thinner and his pallor paler. Steph, on the other hand, looked almost serene.

On the remaining sofa sat Emma with her toes resting in Brad's lap. The young couple were clearly unconcerned that they had bagged front row seats for the denouement of a crime perpetrated against a friend whose generosity they had been more than happy to accept.

Matt and Mia sat separate from the group on a couple of bar stools at the end of the kitchen counter. Rosie appreciated the encouraging smiles and vibes of positivity they were sending her way. When she had spoken to her sister that morning to tell her about what she and Matt had uncovered, Georgina had begged her to delay the 'big reveal' until she drove over to Willerby, as though it was some kind of DIY makeover project. Rosie had smiled at her excitement and promised to recount every tiny detail when she arrived with Jack for the Autumn Leaves party on Saturday night.

Thanks for coming over to the café this morning, everyone,"
began Rosie, nerves gnawing at her abdomen and causing her
to feel lightheaded. For a moment, she wanted to hand over
the revelation baton to Matt, until she looked at the two police
officers, their eyebrows raised as if to say 'Get on with it'.

'Well, come on then! We haven't got all day. I want the
scumbag who did this to me arrested and removed from my
sight!' snapped Rick, sending Helen a look of pure malice for
choosing not to sit next to him whilst the revelations took
place. Every eye in the room swung towards Helen who didn't
help her case by turning a vivid crimson.

'Mr Forster, please,' snapped DS Kirkham, his deep voice
booming through the café. 'If you are unable to control your
emotions, I shall have to ask you to leave. Miss Barnes, if you
wouldn't mind?'

Rosie experienced a sudden surge of confidence, her brain
cleared of all ancillary clutter and she was able to see the
scene she was about to paint as focussed and as clear as a
photograph. Just as Matt had urged, she channelled her inner
Poirot, sent up a quick message of thanks to her father, and
launched in.

'At around seven-thirty on Monday morning, Rick was
found unconscious in the cloister of the Garside Priory with
an arrow imbedded in his ankle. To begin with, we thought
the person responsible had to be a random stranger – possibly
someone who had taken umbrage over our invasion of the
medieval site – because no one from our wild camping group
could have left without one of us noticing their absence.

However, we realized there was an explanation for why we didn't see Rick, or anyone else, leave the site.'

Rosie shot a look at DS Kirkham who stepped forward, his notebook open.

'We analysed the mugs that were used for your final coffee on Sunday evening and found traces of a very strong sedative. Someone in the group needed to make sure everyone slept through Matt's wake-up call.'

'At first, we suspected it to be the work of Rick himself,' continued Rosie, getting into her stride.

'Slander! I must protest in the strongest...'

'Mr Forster, this is your final warning.'

'...that he decided to do it either as a practical joke, or as a selfish act to exclude everyone in his party from witnessing the amazing experience of seeing a new dawn break through the ancient stone arch. But we now know Rick is innocent and the sedative was administered for a much more sinister purpose – in preparation of his murder.'

Shock ricocheted through the café as the group looked at each other and drew closer to the person they were sitting next to for support.

'Are you serious?' asked Steph, her voice quivering in disbelief.

'Absolutely serious. Our intrepid archer was careful to ensure that no sedative found its way into Rick's drink because they knew he intended to set his own alarm an hour earlier than everyone else's. It's no secret how devious he is, how he enjoys getting one over on the rest of the group, especially Phil and Brad, and they played this to their advantage, waiting until he'd left the camp and then following him whilst everyone was out for the count.

'Rick was shot in the ankle, but we can assume because it was a second attempt, that the assailant was aiming for the chest. Of course, the police recovered both arrows, but after an exhaustive search, there was no sign of the bow. This was found yesterday in a hollowed out oak tree in the woods surrounding the camp site by a group of amateur detectorists. Clearly the perpetrator had meticulously planned their assignment in advance, visiting the site to conceal the weapon days, if not weeks, before the wild camping trip. Again, any one of you could have done so.'

'DS Kirkham, correct me if I'm wrong, but is Rosie suggesting that we all could have gone out, purchased a bow and a quiver full of arrows, and simply turned up to kill Rick?' asked Phil, speaking for the first time since he'd arrived at the café. 'Because I can assure you I wouldn't know one end of a longbow from the other.'

'It wasn't a longbow that was used. It was a recurve bow which can be dismantled into three pieces – a riser and two limbs – and easily secreted in a small space. But you are correct, Mr Brown, it does take a great deal of skill to hit what was a moving target. Our perpetrator would have had to train for months to gain the necessary expertise. But that's exactly what they did do.'

'Well, that counts me out then, doesn't it?' said Phil, folding his spindly arms across his chest. 'Sports have never been my forte, unless you count word sprints, which I assume in this case you do not?'

The police officer allowed his gaze to linger on Phil for a while, refusing to confirm or deny that he was on his list of suspects. Phil's eyes swung to Rosie, his spectacles hanging on the end of his nose giving the impression of an anorexic owl as he silently beseeched her to discount him.

'I really must...' began Phil, but when he saw the look on the sergeant's face, he pursed his lips, surreptitiously removed his notebook from one of his many pockets, and started to jot down notes, his leg swinging to and fro over his knee.

'So, is someone going to get to the point and tell us who did this to Rick?' asked Helen, her appearance as polished as always despite the stress of the situation. That morning she had chosen to wear her honey blonde hair in a knot on the top of her head, secured with a diamante clip that glinted in the shards of sunshine spilling through the window behind her. Her powder-blue cashmere sweater reflected her eyes, the colour of bluebells, but her lips were drawn into a narrow line as she waited for the inevitable sword to fall, her hands clutched in her lap, knees and heels drawn together.

'All in good time, Mrs Forster. I'm sure you'll agree that it's important to understand why this happened to your husband, for it is his previous conduct that lies at the crux of the shooting. You, for instance, have a strong motive for wanting him out of the way, don't you?'

Rosie was happy to step back and allow DS Kirkham the floor when Helen squared her shoulders and raised her chin in defiance. She liked Helen, sympathized with her for the years she had spent married to Rick, and didn't want to say anything to upset her any more than was necessary.

'That may be true, Sergeant. I admit that I *have* fallen out of love with my husband, but I would never wish him to come to any harm.'

'Ah, but you stand to gain the most from his potential demise in several ways. Financially, you would inherit his sizeable estate. Three million pounds is not to be sneered at, is it?'

The collective intake of breath would have been comical had the matter not been so serious. Helen's face and chest glowed with heat but she maintained eye contact with the sergeant, and refused to look in the direction of a gobsmacked Rick.

'I have no interest in Rick's money.'

'Really?' spluttered Rick, clearly unable to help himself.

'Maybe not,' DS Kirkham pressed on to prevent Rick from embarking on a diatribe of disbelief. 'But Mr Forster's death would certainly have saved you the trouble of becoming embroiled in lengthy and expensive divorce proceedings. Knowing the way Mr Forster conducts every other aspect of his life, I'm sure he would take a great deal of pleasure in dragging out any financial negotiations, maybe electing to have a contested hearing so that the details of your affair with his business partner could be aired in court. I know that isn't something you want, especially if you are hoping to remarry quickly.'

'My business partner? *Remarry?*' Rick gasped, raising himself up from his wheelchair, his face flooded with thunderous fury. 'What the hell is he talking about, Helen?'

DS Kirkham signalled to his detective constable to station

himself next to Rick until he reluctantly slumped back down in his seat. Helen averted her eyes, suddenly finding her scarlet nail polish fascinating.

'I'm sorry to be the one to inform you, but Mrs Forster has been conducting an affair with one of your partners, Tim Latimer. He is currently staying at a guest house in Willerby and they were together on Sunday night when you were shot.'

DS Kirkham paused to let the disclosure sink in.

'Helen? Is this true?'

Helen nodded.

'Oh my God! Wait until I...'

'Mr Forster, I understand how difficult this is for you to hear, but do you think you could you bear with us for a little while longer?'

Rick stared at the police officer for several beats before nodding his head.

'Maybe Mrs Forster is our perpetrator,' suggested DS Kirkham, his silver eyebrows raised as he surveyed the room. 'She could have easily driven to Garside Priory, recovered the bow she had concealed a few weeks earlier, and shot her husband – Mr Latimer giving her an alibi.'

'I didn't shoot Rick, Sergeant, and neither did Tim. As I've said, I'm not interested in my husband's money. It means nothing compared to my craving for a child, which is something Rick has consistently denied me throughout our marriage. Tim, however, is keen to have a family and I hope I will be blessed with a baby before it's too late.'

Helen's emotions escaped their tethers and tears spilled silently down her cheeks. She dabbed at them with a scrap of lace until Steph crouched down at her side, took her hand and whispered soft words of understanding.

'However,' continued DS Kirkham at last. 'My colleagues have found no evidence to suggest that either of your vehicles were in the vicinity of Garside Priory that night. Mr Latimer has been frank with us about the affair and his statement has checked out. I don't think either of you are responsible for shooting your husband, Mrs Forster.'

Helen blew her nose loudly and inhaled several deep, rejuvenating breaths before refocusing her attention on the police officer.

'Then would you mind telling us all who did?'

'That is precisely what I intend to do, in due course.'

DS Kirkham's gaze came to rest on the sofa where Brad and Emma were watching the proceedings, their jaws hanging loose in avid fascination. The smile on Brad's face slipped and his eyes darted to Rick and then Phil. He removed his ankle from his thigh, unwound his arm from Emma's shoulders and pushed himself to the edge of his seat, placing his forearms on his knees and tilting his head upwards to look Rosie in the eye.

'Don't look at me like that. I've done some stupid things recently, but I didn't shoot Rick.'

Chapter 21

'But you had a good reason to want him out of the way, didn't you?' said Rosie after receiving a nod from DS Kirkham to indicate that she should continue with the explanation.

'Well, I ... I suppose I...'

Again, Brad shot a flash of concern in Rick's direction.

'Rick told you he intended to make a decision this week whether to report your money-making scheme to the police, didn't he?'

'What money-making scheme?' asked Phil, his head swivelling from Rosie to Brad and finally Steph who simply shrugged her shoulders and shook her head.

'Despite Rick generously financing the cost of the Myth Seekers Society's trips abroad to chase down exotic myths and legends, Brad still struggled to afford the ancillary expenses.'

'What do you mean?'

'I mean that Brad helped himself to a souvenir from all the ancient monuments he visited to sell on the internet when he got back home so he could use the cash to finance his next trip. And Emma's. She knew what he was doing, in fact she encouraged it.' Rosie met her eyes. 'Didn't you? Even when Brad's conscience started to twinge.'

'No, I didn't,' snapped Emma, refusing to look at Rosie.

'So you had a nice little sideline going,' spluttered Phil, his eyes filled with dismay. 'Did you also join an archery club to hone your shooting techniques?'

'Look, Phil, you've got to believe me.' Brad turned his widened eyes in the direction of the treasurer of the Myth Seekers Society. It was clear from his expression how desperate he was to explain himself and to seek forgiveness and reassurance that his place amongst the members of the club was still safe. 'I wouldn't shoot Rick, or anyone else for that matter! I'm so, so sorry I did those terrible things. For what it's worth, I did tell Emma that Athens was the last time, didn't I, Em?'

Emma shrugged.

'If that's true, why did we find a chisel with your fingerprints on it up at the Garside Priory?'

'A chisel?' gasped Phil.

'I wasn't going to use it! It was still in my rucksack from our weekend away on the Isle of Man. I promise you. And Phil, you of all people should know that I could never hurt anyone, don't you?' Brad's eyes were pleading now, sending Rosie's heart ballooning in sorrow as she recalled the trauma Brad and his family had suffered.

Phil let out a heavy sigh and shook his head, clearly as distressed as Brad was. 'I know Brad, I know you wouldn't. Sergeant? Are you accusing Brad of shooting Rick or not?'

'Mr Cookson could have easily introduced the sedative to your drinking water on his way back from the stream, then waited until everyone was asleep, followed Rick on his hike up to the priory and shot him with the bow and arrow he had hidden in a carved-out tree trunk a few weeks before. If Rick had died, Brad's crimes would never be reported and his continued membership of the Myth Seekers Society would not be in jeopardy.'

'But I didn't do it!' cried Brad, standing up from his seat, his face scarlet, his fists clenched at his thighs.

The uniformed officer stepped forward from his station at the French doors, but DS Kirkham held up his palm. 'Sit down, Mr Cookson, I know you are not responsible for shooting Mr Forster.' He shifted his concentration to Emma. He let his eyes rest on the top of her head until she glanced up to see him staring at her.

'Don't look at me! I didn't shoot Rick either! Why would I do such a thing, I hardly know him!'

'You met Mr Forster for the first time when you joined the Myth Seekers Society, is that right?'

'Yes, but I saw how Rick went on with Phil and some of the other older member so I decided from the outset to steer clear of his brand of intimidation.'

'But you were happy to accept his financial contribution to your trips abroad?'

'Sure, we all were. It isn't a reason to shoot him though, is it? In fact, it's quite the opposite, wouldn't you say? I don't think we'll be going abroad again any time soon. And before you ask, Rick wasn't threatening me with anything either.'

'No, I don't suppose he was. So that leaves us with Mr and Mrs Brown.'

'Now wait a minute, Sergeant...' began Steph, raising her buttocks from her seat on the sofa, her hands on her hips. Her sunflower-bedecked tea dress, tightened at her narrow waist with a twisted rope belt, lent her the air of a Fifties TV presenter. She dragged the sides of her mustard coloured cardigan across her chest and crossed her arms before meeting the officer's eyes head on.

'Please sit down, Mrs Brown.'

Steph looked down at her husband, rolled her eyes at his inaction and did as requested, smoothing her skirt over her knees.

'Perhaps unforeseeably, you were alone at the lodges on Sunday night. You could have raced over to Garside Priory, shot Mr Forster and returned without anyone noticing your absence. However,' the sergeant hurried on as he saw Steph's lips begin to part in indignation, 'there is no way you could have introduced the sedative to the evening coffee unless acting in partnership with someone else, such as your husband.'

'Sergeant Kirkham, I really must...'

'If you would do me the courtesy of hearing me out, Mrs Brown.'

Steph lapsed into angry silence, her eyes narrowed, her brow creased as she stared at him with patent dislike. Rosie saw the sergeant give her a nod and she took up the narrative.

'I think everyone here knew that Phil wanted to invest in a plaque to commemorate the Myth Seekers Society's twentieth anniversary. When he presented the resolution to the committee it was voted down by Rick. Phil was really upset, so he went ahead and ordered it anyway, taking the funds from the accounts without permission.'

'Good on you, Phil. You have my total support!' cried Brad, before sinking back into the folds of the sofa, clearly regretting sticking his head above the parapet.

'Unfortunately, Rick wasn't quite so forgiving and he threatened to report the matter not only to the members, but to the local police.'

'Perhaps you panicked?' continued Detective Sergeant Kirkham. 'Or maybe Mr Forster's perpetual line in sarcastic comments became just too much this weekend. You snapped and decided to remove him from your life once and for all? You could have easily added the sedative to the coffee. You could have followed your tormentor's trek to the priory, maybe to challenge him over his selfish desire to exclude the other members from enjoying the experience of watching the sunrise. However, as I said before, this incident was premeditated, not something that was committed after a spur of the moment loss of control. The perpetrator had to have planned this months ago so that the bow and arrow could be hidden, ready to be retrieved at the opportune moment and returned afterwards.'

'So, Sergeant,' interrupted Helen, glaring at him as if he was solely responsible for preventing her imminent escape to her new life. 'We've just been told that someone in this room intended to murder Rick by shooting him with an arrow and then both you and Rosie have gone on to discount every one of us? Oh, unless...'

Helen's eyes lingered on Matt for a few brief seconds

before moving to Mia who had the brazenness to give her her most vibrant smile until she looked away embarrassed. The creases at the side of DS Kirkham's lips tightened as he sent a silent signal to Matt and his officer stationed at the French door.

'Mr Forster's shooting had nothing to do with his membership of the Myth Seekers Society. Nor did it have anything to do with his malicious behaviour towards its members or his threats to expose Brad and Phil for their misdemeanours. The assault on his life was carefully planned over many years, as resentment built into a hatred so intense that the only release for the perpetrator was the commission of such a heinous act.'

DS Kirkham now had everyone's full attention; every eye in the Windmill Café was focused on his face. Rosie could feel her heart thumping against her ribcage as she waited for him to reveal the identity of the culprit. For all her involvement, for all the time and effort she had invested in trawling through the facts she had helped to uncover, for all her reliance on her gut reaction, her intuition, her instinct, to lead her and Matt to their discoveries, she would not want to be standing in DS Kirkham's shoes at that moment. Neither would Matt, as he'd shown when he'd been asked whether he would like to announce the name of the person responsible for shooting Rick.

Rosie understood exactly how Matt felt – that person had almost destroyed the outward-bound business his father had founded and guided to success, they'd almost destroyed not only his livelihood but that of Freddie and Mia too. She could see the sparks of fury flying behind his eyes as he waited for the sergeant to reveal all.

'Permit me tell you how it happened. We know that the assailant had to make sure the group slept through Matt's wake-up call so a sedative was administered by way of the coffee, except for their own and their victim's. When Mr Forster woke up, he set off to Garside Priory to appreciate the sunrise solo. His attacker waited until he was at a safe distance before following him, collecting their bow and quiver from its hiding place on the way.

'Our archer waited until Mr Forster entered the cloister, took aim and released their first arrow, which missed. I believe nerves played a part in this lack of accuracy, and the error gave Mr Forster the chance to run towards safety whilst the bow was being rearmed. It's much more difficult to hit a moving target, and the second attempt only managed to pierce their victim's ankle before he gained shelter. Anxious not to draw attention to their absence, our perpetrator replaced the bow in the tree trunk and sprinted back to camp. What a perfect alibi, to be able to awake with the rest of the group and declare themselves disgusted at Mr Forster's betrayal.'

Detective Sergeant Kirkham paused for a few moments to let the facts sink in, before continuing 'However, our intrepid archer hadn't bargained on the curiosity and puzzle-solving abilities of our local crime-busting duo. Rosie and Matt had started to ask questions and come up with a few answers, some of which were just a little close for comfort, so it was imperative to warn them off. The message was made loud and clear by gaining access to Rosie's bedroom and leaving a calling card by way of an arrow in one of her soft toys. Fortunately, this did nothing to deter their investigation.'

DS Kirkham dark-pewter eyes roamed around the room like a laser beam, until they stopped and honed in on one individual.

'That was what you did, wasn't it?' Again, a short, dramatic pause. 'Emma?'

A collective gasp of surprise rippled around the room as every pair of eyes swung to look at her. For the first time since they had arrived at the café, not a single word escaped from Rick's mouth, but the shock was evident across his expression. Emma, however, was highly vocal, leaping up from her seat to make herself heard all the more.

'What? No way! Why are you saying that? Why would I want to shoot Rick? I told you, I hardly even knew him!'

Emma pivoted her head from left to right seeking support for her denial from Brad, then Phil and Steph. Her face had drained of all colour and her eyes were wide with indignation and disbelief. But Rosie spotted a tremble in her fingertips and tiny beads of perspiration at her temples.

'Because, Miss Hewitt,' continued DS Kirkham, slipping his hand into his jacket pocket to extract a length of cream parchment, 'Richard John Forster is your father.'

'He's your father?' gasped Brad, his jaw loose, flicking his eyes over to a white-faced Rick, whose earlier arrogance and irritation at the proceedings had seeped from his face like candlewax.

'Yes, Mr Cookson. Richard Forster is the father who abandoned Emma and her mother within weeks of her birth, forcing her mother to struggle through job after job to make ends meet as a single parent. It all became too much for her, didn't it, Emma? She committed suicide when you were ten years old. You went to live with your aunt and cousins but you never forgave your father for what he did.'

'Look, Sergeant, I don't know what you're...'

The police officer stepped forward to lay the birth certificate on Emma's knees, holding her eyes with his, waiting until she glanced down at the spidery handwriting, at the evidence that stated irrefutably that Richard John Forster was Emma Jayne Hewitt's father.

'You blame Richard Forster for your mother's untimely death and for that he had to pay. I suspect that when you were eighteen you decided to search for him. When you eventually found him, and saw how well he'd done for himself, it could only have hardened your resolve. You began to gather as much information as you could about his life and his activities and a plan formulated in your mind. Then you discovered he was the chairman of the Myth Seekers Society and decided to join. What better way to watch him more closely, find out what sort of man he really was. There was no chance he would recognize you, you were only a few weeks old when he last saw you and he'd never followed your progress through life or offered to pay any child support. Perhaps if he had, we wouldn't be in this position today.'

'Emma...'

'You latched on to Brad, used your relationship with him to join the foreign trips so you could continue your surveillance of the life Richard Forster had made for himself after leaving your mother, watch him splash the money he'd earned whilst your mother struggled to feed and clothe you. Resentment festered and your plan fell into place.'

'Emma? What is he saying?' demanded Brad, his voice wavering as he moved away from her to the end of the sofa they shared, his upper lip beginning to curl in revulsion.

'It's all a load of bullshit, Brad. Don't listen to him,' Emma spat as she flung the birth certificate onto the floor and reached over to fold Brad's hand into hers. But he pushed her away, stood up and moved to sit on a bar stool at the kitchen counter between Matt and Mia.

'We have Miss Barnes here to thank for unearthing the evidence that you took part in a taster course offered by the Cheshire Archery Association at the gym where you work. And whilst I suspect you used a false name to sign up for the residential archery course that was held in North Wales last summer, your image is on a photograph of everyone who passed the course – and we also have a statement from one of the instructors who coached you and he's prepared to give evidence to that effect. He confirmed that you shoot a recurve bow exactly like the one we found in the woods at Garside.'

Emma stared at Rick, her fingers raking through her hair, her demeanour agitated. She paused, as if preparing to take flight, and then her eyes ignited with passion and she launched herself at Rick.

'I hate you!' she screamed, her fists flying high as she rained down punches on her father until an appalled Steph helped the detective constable to settle her back onto the sofa. 'If you hadn't walked out on Mum after I was born she would still be alive! Have you any idea how hard it is to stand at your mother's grave when you're ten years old? Nothing, nothing at all can stop the agony – or even begin to heal the pain. Nothing!'

Tears streamed down Emma's cheeks and her green eyes, so reminiscent of Rick's, flashed around the gathering as she challenged each one of them to disagree with her. Rosie knew *she* couldn't – she knew exactly what it felt like to lose a parent. In fact, if she were honest, in those dark days and weeks after her father's death she had also considered marching into his law firm to harangue the people responsible for making him work so hard that he'd suffered a fatal heart attack. But, unlike Emma, she had been lucky enough to have her mother, and her sister, to stand by her side as she railed against life's cruelty and to guide her away from her brief flirtation with insanity.

She stared at the broken young girl curled into a ball in the corner of the sofa, her eyes wild, her fists pressed into her mouth, her slender body convulsed with the pain of her memories, as DS Kirkham approached her. At the same time, Helen rose from her chair and went to sit beside Emma. She hooked her arm around her shoulders and the girl began to keen for the still-raw loss of her mother, rocking backwards and forwards like a wounded animal.

'I'm so sorry for what Rick did to you,' Helen whispered, her own tears falling unchecked. 'He told me he had a child from his first marriage. I should have taken more interest, should have tried to find you. I was so wrapped up in myself and my desire to have a baby of my own – it was all I could think about. I'll engage a decent criminal lawyer to represent you, Emma, from my divorce settlement. It's the least I can do.'

Emma lifted her eyes to look at Helen with incredulity, her breath coming in gulps.

'Really? You'll do that?'

'Come with me, please, Miss Hewitt,' said DS Kirkham, holding out his hand to guide Emma from the room.

Emma slowly pushed herself from the sofa, shooting a final glance at Brad who averted his eyes, after which she allowed herself to be handcuffed and lead from the café.

'I'm going with her,' announced Helen, and without a backward glance at a very shocked Rick, she strode from the room to catch up with Emma and the police officers.

The atmosphere in the café crackled with charged emotions. However, far from averting their eyes, everyone was staring at Rick with distaste. Rosie had expected the chairman of the Myth Seekers Society to immediately launch into a lecture of conceited self-justification, but Rick wasn't totally insensitive. He had no doubt realized he would be preaching to a hostile audience and had decided to remain silent. In fact, perhaps there was even a little shame lurking behind his pale green eyes.

The discomfort continued to swirl around the room until Rick announced he was leaving and a whoosh of relief broke the tension, which in itself caused two dots of heat to appear on Rick's cheeks. Rosie suspected Rick had attended his last Myth Seekers meeting. She watched as he wheeled himself out to the terrace and struggled to make speedy progress along the gravelled pathway, calling over his shoulder, 'Send your invoice to my office, Rosie, if you please.'

'Of course.'

Rosie smiled briefly at Matt and Mia as they joined her outside the Windmill Café. She watched the police 4X4 disappear down the driveway, her chest alive with a cauldron of sensations. Whilst she was relieved they had uncovered the identity of Rick's attacker, Emma's story had been a profoundly sorrowful one that she wouldn't wish on anyone and she hoped that the circumstances of her actions would be taken into account at her trial.

She heaved a sigh and raised her eyes to the sky. Dusk had begun to send ribbons of indigo, violet and salmon pink across the canopy overhead, but she ignored its attempt at beauty in the face of such sadness. No one in the little Windmill Café had spoken since Rick had departed; each lost in their own thoughts as they tried to assimilate everything they had just heard into some kind of order they could understand.

'I think we could all do with a drink.'

Rosie put the kettle to boil and Mia helped set out the teapot, the cafetière and a random selection of china mugs and cups. Matt fetched a bottle of whiskey from his SUV, whilst Rosie arranged a selection of the cakes and pastries she and Mia had baked on Sunday afternoon – a lifetime ago, but in reality, only four days ago.

Yet in that time everything had changed for all the guests in the Windmill Café's lodges.

Chapter 22

'Thank goodness everyone's enjoying themselves,' sighed Rosie, setting down her glass of warm cinnamon-spiced mulled wine and reaching for one of Mia's scull-shaped ginger biscuits decorated in crimson icing.

'You can say that again,' agreed Matt. 'Rumours of a murderer on the loose stalking ramblers, hikers and myth seekers isn't the best marketing plan for the businesses in the area who rely on tourism. I'm happy to report, however, that the people who cancelled their courses have all rebooked and we've had more enquiries since that piece written by Dan Forrester was syndicated.'

'Does that mean my job as a zip wire instructor is definitely safe?' smiled Mia, tucking into a fluffy marshmallow ghost.

'It certainly is. Monday morning, 8 a.m. sharp. No excuses, Miss Williams.'

'Yes, sir!' Mia saluted Matt and then collapsed into giggles. 'Don't worry, Rosie, I'll still be helping out at the Windmill Café at weekends, and I'm really excited about the Christmas tree-decorating competition in December. You can't get rid of me that easily.'

'I'm relieved to hear it, Mia. How Graham expects me to run the café single-handedly is beyond me. I know we'll only be open on Saturdays and Sundays from now until March, but we'll still be as busy as ever – and I'll miss you!'

'Is anyone left in the lodges?'

'No, everyone went home last night. No one wanted to hang around after the police left. Helen rang me from Norwich police station to ask me to pack up her belongings and when I went over to her lodge, Rick was surprisingly accommodating. Freddie's promised to drive up to Manchester and drop everything off at Tim's house for her.'

'What about Brad? He must be devastated.'

'I'm not sure how he's feeling, to be honest. He apologized to Phil and Steph for his lapse in integrity over the artefact thefts and promised it would never happen again. Phil suggested Brad might like to become their social secretary just to underline how much they value his membership, but I don't think the Myth Seekers Society will be arranging any foreign trips for a while. One good thing to come out of all this is that Brad told me he intends to spend more time with his parents because he appreciates how much they must miss him, especially without his brother around. I'm not sure he'll be telling them his ex-girlfriend was a potential murderer, though.'

'What about Phil?'

'He's promised to spend some of the society's funds on attracting new, younger members so Brad feels more at home. And, he's not planning on finishing his second book on folklore because he's started on a first draft of a crime novel, would you believe? Set on the Norfolk Broads!' Rosie laughed. That was one book she intended to pre-order as soon as it was available. 'Apparently Helen's engaged one of Norfolk's top criminal defence lawyers to represent Emma. I don't know what the outcome will be for her but at least she will get the opportunity to present her case.'

'Is that a twinkle of envy in your eye?' smiled Matt, sending Mia a covert glance over the rim of his glass that had the banned eyeballs floating on the surface.

'What are you two cooking up?' asked Rosie suspiciously.

'Well, we know how much you wanted to follow in your father's legalistic footsteps, so we just thought you might like to consider this,' said Matt, producing a glossy prospectus for the local college and handing it over to Rosie, his blue eyes holding hers, sending a delicious spasm of pleasure swirling around her body. 'I've marked the page.'

Rosie took the brochure from Matt and opened it, her heart performing a flip-flop of excitement when she realized what her friends were suggesting.

'Oh my God! Are you serious?'

'Totally!' declared Mia, stepping forward to hug Rosie. 'I've spoken to Mum. She knows the lecturer who teaches on the A level law course and he says it's the perfect option. I know it's not a degree, but it's a start.'

'Oh, Matt, Mia, that's so thoughtful of you. Thank you,' she just about managed to say as gratitude tightened her throat, but a kernel of anticipation and potential new beginnings had imbedded in her mind where she knew it would germinate. Could she?

'It's never too late to chase your dreams, Rosie. And I'm going to start with a slice of that Boston Scream pie over there.' Matt drained his glass and made his way through the chattering throng of guests at the Autumn Leaves party to the makeshift bar where Graham, recently arrived back from his sojourn on his brother's yacht in Palma harbour, was rushed off his feet.

'So, have you and Matt talked any more about going to Grace and Josh's wedding together?'

'No, but it does seem like a great idea,' said Rosie, her cheeks flushing with heat at her admission for the first time that there was more than friendship brewing between them. Happiness blossomed as she thought of standing next to Matt in the church whilst their friends exchanged their vows.

'I happen to think you are perfect for each other, and maybe a wedding is the ideal opportunity for you to get together as a couple.'

'Mia...'

'Just giving the path of true love a little gentle nudge in the right direction,' Mia giggled, taking another sip of the lethal blood-coloured punch that she and Freddie had concocted. 'You've got to admit Matt is not only handsome, he's also incredibly sexy in that rugged, outdoorsy kind of way. If you could both try not to attract any more chaos into your lives, I think things will run a lot smoother from now on. Willerby has never seen so much excitement since you landed on our doorstep, Rosie Barnes.'

A shadow fell over their table on the terrace outside the Windmill Café and Rosie looked up, a wide smile on her face, ready to tell Matt she'd be delighted to be his plus one for Grace and Josh's nuptials. But it wasn't Matt.

'Ah, Rosie, there you are. I hope you don't mind me dropping in on you without an invitation. Looks like a great party! I'm loving this Hallowe'en punch, but I don't think I should drive anywhere afterwards, do you?'

Rosie stared at the man standing in front of her, a man she thought she would never set eyes on again – and certainly hoped never to set eyes on again. Her heart had escaped its moorings and jumped into her throat where it continued to flap and flutter as she struggled to understand what her eyes and ears were forcing her to believe.

'Harry? What on earth are you doing here?'

'Well, it's probably not the best venue to discuss this, but I've come to make amends and take you back to London.'

'Harry, I don't want...'

'What's going on, Rosie?' said Matt, appearing on the terrace, holding a tray of drinks. 'Are you okay?'

'Of course she's okay. Or she will be in just a few seconds,' announced Harry, frowning at Matt as he fiddled to find something in his jacket pocket.

As Rosie watched on in horror, Harry produced a black velvet box, lowered himself down onto one knee and met her eyes.

'Rosalina Catherine Barnes, will you marry me?'

Acknowledgements

A completed novel is always the result of a team effort, so I would like to say a huge, heartfelt thank you to the wonderful team at HarperImpulse, in particular my editor, Charlotte Ledger, for helping me make The Windmill Café series the best it can be.

HELP US SHARE THE LOVE!

If you love this wonderful book as much as we do then please share your reviews online.

Leaving reviews makes a huge difference and helps our books reach even more readers.

So get reviewing and sharing, we want to hear what you think!

Love, HarperImpulse x

Please leave your reviews online!

amazon.co.uk   kobo   goodreads   L♥vereading   iBooks

And on social!

f/HarperImpulse   🐦@harperimpulse
📷@HarperImpulse

LOVE BOOKS?

So do we! And we love nothing more than chatting about our books with you lovely readers.

If you'd like to find out about our latest titles, as well as exclusive competitions, author interviews, offers and lots more, join us on our Facebook page! Why not leave a note on our wall to tell us what you thought of this book or what you'd like to see us publish more of?

f/HarperImpulse

You can also tweet us 🐦@harperimpulse and see exclusively behind the scenes on our Instagram page www.instagram.com/harperimpulse

To be the first to know about upcoming books and events, sign up to our newsletter at: www.harperimpulseromance.com